F. E. Head

Faithful in little

A Tale for young Women

F. E. Head

Faithful in little
A Tale for young Women

ISBN/EAN: 9783337082345

Printed in Europe, USA, Canada, Australia, Japan

Cover: Foto ©Andreas Hilbeck / pixelio.de

More available books at **www.hansebooks.com**

FAITHFUL IN LITTLE.

MRS. WILSON'S PARTING PRESENT.

BY

MRS. F. E. HEAD.

FOURTH EDITION.

LONDON:

JARROLD & SONS, 3, PATERNOSTER BUILDINGS.

CONTENTS.

PART THE FIRST.

THE SERVANT.

FAITHFUL IN LITTLE.

PART THE FIRST.

THE SERVANT.

IVE and thirty years ago, a young girl knocked timidly at a door in Finsbury Place, about seven o'clock on a winter's evening. She was evidently expected, or in so noisy a place her knock would hardly have attracted any notice. The door was speedily opened by a young lady, who said, "Come in, Jane, we have been expecting you." The tone of voice was particularly pleasant, and seemed to encourage the girl, who entered at once, and, placing a bandbox she had carried in her hand on the mat in the passage, turned to help a man with a box, which was also placed within the door. The man departed and the door was closed, and thus Jane Stimpson

entered Mrs. Wilson's service as maid-of-all-work
to her and her three daughters, who occupied part
of a house in that noisy part of London which has
been mentioned.

I must try and describe Jane as she looked on
this, to her, memorable evening. Fancy a hungry-
looking girl of sixteen, with a very doughy complexion, hair of no particular colour, rather short
in stature, with an old look for her years, and you
will have a tolerable notion of Jane's appearance,
and will perceive that she was certainly no beauty.
But if she had not beauty, she seemed honest and
looked you straight in the face when spoken to,
and her eyes brightened wonderfully when addressed in terms of kindness. In fact, it was the
expression of her face, joined to a tolerably fair
character, that had induced Mrs. Wilson to engage
her, as she was so very young for such a place ; but
she had begged so earnestly of that lady "only to
try her," for she "was sure she should be able to
do," and was not to be daunted by the number of
stairs or any of the manifold discomforts of a London place-of-all-work. So Jane was installed ; and
after the first novelty was worn off, and she became
somewhat accustomed to her situation, she showed
herself apt in learning her duties. At first, her
notions of arranging the furniture were decidedly

original, and afforded her young mistresses great amusement; laying the cloth properly for dinner was an important business, and her look of dismay when she discovered that there were no spoons on the table or she had forgotten the tumblers, was almost comic. But Jane had the will to do, and she soon found the way, and very rarely forgot when she once thoroughly understood any direction. Mrs. Wilson was a particularly kind-hearted lady, with a very pleasant expression of face. She held a firm rule over the house, and neither her daughters nor servant would have dreamed of disobeying her wishes; but she was so good and thoughtful that they all loved her very dearly, and Jane looked up to her with infinite respect. Jane soon learned to love the young ladies, but especially the eldest, who was in rather delicate health. Miss Wilson and her sister, Miss Dora, had daily pupils, who occupied them during the morning; and the youngest, Miss Mary, was studying hard to be fitted to help her sisters. The family were very happy together, and though they led a quiet life they were very cheerful and merry, and treated Jane with more kindness than she had ever had shown her in her life. Her naturally kind and good nature seemed to expand in so genial an atmosphere, as, indeed, most natures do.

Jane had not been with Mrs. Wilson long, when
Miss Wilson was taken ill, and was confined to her
bed for some time. This illness added a great deal
to the work, the kitchen being underground, as it
generally is in London houses, and Miss Wilson's
room at the top of the house, which was four stories
high. Jane's poor legs must have often ached with
the constant running up and downstairs ; but she
took such a true interest in the patient that she
made light of trouble, and proved a most pains-
taking and affectionate assistant in the sick room.
When Miss Wilson was getting a little better and
sat up, Jane was very proud to be allowed to stay
in her room and talk to her, and then, bit by bit,
came out some of the trials of her former life. She
was born in a close court in the city. Her father,
who was a bricklayer, had been killed by falling
from a scaffold, leaving her mother a widow with
Jane and a younger sister, both quite babies. The
mother struggled on as well as she could, going out
charing ; and Jane spoke of the long days when
she and her little sister were left locked up in a
garret by themselves ; and how cold it was in the
winter, when they had no fire for fear of their
getting burnt. Then, how when she was old
enough she got a little place to mind a baby, and
her mistress was a harsh, ill-tempered woman, who

would beat her on the smallest pretence, and kept her very short of food ; but, " The baby was such a dear, miss, and was so fond of me, that I was quite sorry when he ran alone, and missus said she couldn't keep me any longer doing nothing." Then she got a place in a lodging-house, in a dreadfully close neighbourhood, where she had to sleep in the back kitchen close to the sink. Often and often she was not in bed before midnight, and up again before six, and what scraps of food she had, she had barely time to eat ! No wonder her growth was so stunted, poor child ! Willing as she was to do her best, she could not stand the work ; she caught a fever, and had to be taken to the hospital. This illness and being in the hospital was evidently the portion of her short life that she looked back upon as a kind of holiday, the only one she had ever known. " To be sure, miss, I was very bad and knowed nothing for a long time ; but after a bit I got to know things, and it was so nice to lie there so comfortable and have nice things, and the doctor was very kind and quite a grand-looking gentle-man, and nurse Blore was so good to me."

" Yes, indeed," said Miss Wilson," " getting well is, as you say, very nice, Jane ; and I am very thankful to feel a good deal stronger to-day than I have been since I was laid up. You have been a good little nurse, and I think you learnt something from being ill yourself. Our Father in heaven always sends some good to His children even in what seems bad at the time. Your being ill taught you how nice kindness is to the sick, and that is a good lesson to any one, and worth being ill to learn."

"Please, miss," said Jane, "that is just what the chaplain at the hospital told me one day; and I think he said that God lets us be ill sometimes, perhaps, that we might think of Him more. The chaplain would come into the ward, and read such beautiful stories out of the Bible, about Jesus healing the poor sick people."

"They are beautiful stories, indeed," said Miss Wilson; "and those stories of our Saviour always seem to be more beautiful and comforting when we are sick or in sorrow. When we are weak we want love and kindness. Jesus is ever near us, and we feel He knows our wants, and that He can and does hear when we come to Him for help. He knew pain and grief on earth, and He feels for us in our need, and bids us come to Him to be healed."

Jane had not had many opportunities of gaining knowledge, but whenever a little grain of the good seed had fallen in her way, it was lodged in good ground and promised to bring forth abundant fruit, for what she knew she practised.

By dint of a good deal of spelling she could manage to read a little, and as she expressed an earnest desire to improve, Miss Mary undertook to give her lessons. She began to learn writing and arithmetic, very necessary accomplishments. Jane progressed pretty well in her studies, and as soon as she could write a little she was provided with a slate and pencil, on which she was expected to put down an account of the money she spent. This slate was often a source of laughter, for spelling was rather a stumbling-block to Jenny. "Eggs" were invariably "heggs," "cabbages" "cabbags," while "oysters" would have puzzled anyone to decipher. But if her orthography was queer, her accounts were sure to be correct, and that was the more important of the two.

Mrs. Wilson and her daughters were so fully occupied, that Jane had to do a good deal of the marketing; and had she been careless and dishonest, her mistress would have suffered loss she could very ill afford. The tradespeople with whom Mrs. Wilson dealt, soon learnt to know Jane, and always treated her with the kind of respect that is generally accorded even to a young servant girl, if she deserves it.

"A tidy young lass that of Mrs. Wilson's; she has a head on her shoulders. She knows what she wants when she comes into the shop, and looks to see she has it; always counts her change, and neither wastes my young men's time or her own by chattering, as most of the young girls do—aye, and old ones too, for the matter of that. Though she can give them a bit of her mind too. I had a new hand lately," continued Mr. Forster, the cheese-monger, "who of course did not know the girl, and he served her with some bacon that certainly was not quite what I should have thought fit to send Mrs. Wilson. You should have seen her—she wondered where he had lived all his life that he did not know what was fit to send such a lady as her mistress. I happened to hear her, and made peace by serving her myself, and telling the man I hoped he would look out as sharp for my interests as she did for her mistress's."

Jane's wardrobe was very scanty when she first entered Mrs. Wilson's service, though the few clothes she had were whole and clean. Her mistress used to maintain that a great deal of the untidiness and carelessness, or what may be called "shiftlessness," of the poorer class, arises from want of knowledge as well as from want of thought. They see a thing marked up a great bargain in

shop windows, and they are tempted to buy simply
because it is cheap, without considering whether it
is what they want, or whether it is likely to wear
well. Mrs. Wilson often said she wished the word
" cheap " was banished from the dictionary—cheap
things were so often dear.

Jane had at first only six pounds a year—to her
a large sum—and it was quite an event when she
received her first quarter's wages. Her mistress
asked her what she intended to do with her money,
kindly adding that her own time was too much
occupied to allow her to give her much assistance in
spending it ; " but if you consult Miss Ellen, I dare
say she will help you to lay it out better than you
could do by yourself. I can only give you advice,
and you must try and remember that ' to wish ' for
a thing is not really ' to want ' it, and learn to say,
' I can do without it.' "

Miss Wilson was quite willing to superintend
Jane's purchases, and went with her to the draper's
with whom the family generally dealt. It was a
very serious business to lay out thirty shillings to
the best advantage, but Miss Wilson had the happy
art of guiding without appearing to dictate, and the
result of their shopping was a pretty print for a
dress, and aprons, calico, and stockings. There
was some idea of a bonnet to wear on Sundays,

B

and it really was a "want." Jane thought her
shoes would do a little longer; but on examination
she acknowledged that she needed them even more
than the bonnet; so they were bought and paid
for, and the purchase of a bonnet was obliged to be
deferred till next quarter-day. She had about
half-a-crown left, and Miss Wilson advised her to
keep that for any little expenses, as it was not well
to be quite without money in hand. Jane was
rather disappointed about the bonnet, and, swal-
lowing a sigh, exclaimed,

"Law, miss, how fast money does go, to be sure!
But I have a frock now and lots of work to do, and
I shall get some more wages soon, and then I can
get a bonnet."

Miss Wilson gave an account of their marketings
to her sisters on her return home, and told them
how well Jane had given up her desire for a bonnet.

"Poor thing!" said Dora, "it was very good of
her; there is an old straw one of mine, I shall never
wear it again; and if I look out some ribbon, I
daresay I can make it look more tidy than her own,
which certainly does look antiquated."

When the bonnet was nicely retrimmed, Dora
gave it to Jane, who was exceedingly pleased, and
thought her young ladies were, as she said, "very
good to her."

The sisters usually made their own clothes, and after her work was done, Jane was had upstairs and taught how to cut out and fix her own garments. She was an apt pupil, partly because she had such an earnest desire to succeed, and in course of time became a very expert needlewoman.

In a neat bonnet and well-fitting print dress, Jane looked a very different girl from the poor hungry-looking being she was when she first came to Mrs. Wilson's. It was pleasant to hear her singing at her work ; she was very fond of music, and caught up a tune both quickly and correctly.

The great treats of her life were the musical parties that were occasionally held at Mrs. Wilson's; Jane always took care to get through her work with extra speed, that she might take up her place just outside the drawing-room door and listen to the singing, and she had a very correct idea as to the sweetness of this or that particular voice. Her remarks, which were usually confided to Miss Mary, were very amusing, generally terminating with,

" But law ! miss, your mamma do play so beautiful ; and how lovely Miss Ellen did sing that song ! a deal nicer than that Mrs. Brown, who goes up so screechy-like."

So, in truth, Jane lived a happier life than ever before ; not because there were no troubles, but her

happy temper kept her from making them. She
did her best, and who can do more? She knew
her mistress intended her good, so if now and then
she spoke more hastily than was altogether necessary, Jane did not answer pertly, or go downstairs
and grumble to herself and dwell on her grievances.

Mrs. Wilson had a great many troubles and
anxieties, and she worked very hard, and sometimes she might be thought irritable, but Jane
knew that no unkindness was intended. She would
think to herself that " Missus was a bit worrited—I
always knows it when she rings so quick ; but,
laws ! she looked so cold and tired when she comed
in, it ain't no wonder."

Unfortunately for the peace of domestic life, too
many are ready to resent a hasty word, and fre-
quently pride themselves on doing so, as a proof
of spirit, and having a proper regard for themselves,
forgetting, or too often, alas ! having never learned,
that it is " the meek and quiet spirit " which is of
" great price " in the sight of God, and which is also
called an " ornament," and surely is one that can
never get old-fashioned or unsuitable to any station
of life.

Jane was by no means deficient in spirit of the
right kind, and was not always as meek as she
might have been ; but if things went a little

crooked, as things will occasionally do in the best
regulated family, she had no notion of setting them
straight by ill-temper or sulkiness; as she would
say, "What's the use? two wrongs won't make one
right." So she would only try and make things
look brighter, and somehow the brightness downstairs insensibly would ascend upstairs, and not
unfrequently helped to raise spirits that had much
to depress them. Her mistress was of that gene-
rous nature that never failed to be touched by
Jane's forbearance, and though of course nothing
was said, there was none the less felt.

Jane was certainly a comfort in the household,
and the friends of the family all took an interest in
her, and had a kind word for her.

"What a nice expression of face your servant
has!" was a frequent remark. And it was quite
true, because she had the goodness of heart that is
a greater beautifier to the countenance than regular features and a clear complexion.

As time went on, Jane's circumstances mended,
her wages were increased year by year, and so well
had she profited by the advice and assistance of
her young mistress, that she had learnt both to buy
her clothes with judgment, and to make and mend
them well. Acting by Mrs. Wilson's advice, she
began to lay by money in the Savings' Bank, and

very proud was she when she had a whole sovereign in safety there.

"Now you are a woman of property, Jane, you will be getting a sweetheart," said Miss Wilson, "so be careful."

"Oh, miss, that won't be in a hurry, for no one would be like to fall in love with my beauty, and I shan't say nothing of my savings. I won't be married for my money, any way, so there's no fear of me."

Love affairs certainly did occupy Jane's attention a good deal about this time, as the second Miss Wilson was engaged, and of course her intended husband paid frequent visits to the house. Jane thought he was a very nice gentleman; "but then, Miss Dora was such a nice young lady, there wasn't many was good enough for her."

She had an idea that it was not quite right for the second daughter to marry before the eldest: but it was an idea she kept quite to herself, and would have resented it stoutly from anyone else. She loved all her young ladies, but Miss Wilson was the object of her most profound admiration.

In the first place, she had delicate health, and often wanted petting and nursing; and secondly, she had nursed Jane through a sharp illness, and to be nursed by Miss Wilson, who had a natural turn

for the vocation, was rather a luxury than otherwise. Moreover, she was so good-tempered and
loving, that no wonder Jane thought in her heart
that Mr. Lee was a trifle blind. But she made
much of him, notwithstanding, and generally contrived to have something she fancied he liked for
supper when he was expected.

"Jane," said her mistress, "I really cannot afford
four eggs in a rice pudding."

"Law, ma'am, it was only for Mr. Lee, and I
made sure you would not mind, and I heard him
say he did like a nice baked rice pudding; perhaps,
as he lives in lodgings, ma'am, he don't get very
good puddings: leastways, my old missus did not
care much how she cooked for the young gents she
had to lodge, and they used to grumble awful
sometimes, and call the puddings 'stickjaw,' so I
thought gentlemen liked things good."

"Yes, I daresay they do, Jane; but you must
not teach them extravagance, so you must not use
so many eggs again."

"Very well, ma'am," replied Jane; but still the
puddings were as good as ever, and Jane had
always excellent reasons to give for making them,
and of course Miss Dora quite agreed with her that
nothing could be too good or too nice for Mr. Lee.

Mrs. Wilson was considerably amused with Jane's

notions that gentlemen liked good cookery, and
advised her daughter to study the art diligently, for
she would find that domestic comfort and health
depended a great deal on well-cooked food.

"You see, my dear," continued Mrs. Wilson,
"Jane has good common sense and uses it too;
and if ever she has a house of her own, I think she
will make a better housewife than many double her
age. I do not mean to cast any reflections on you,
my child, as I feel quite confident you will study
your husband's comfort; but young people do not
always see what comfort consists in, and are rather
apt to undervalue cookery. The Scotch proverb
of 'a cheerful face and clean hearth-stane' being
pleasant things for a tired man to see on his return
home from business is quite true, and I do not
fancy Alfred will ever miss them in his own home;
but add to them a nicely-appointed table and appe-
tising food, and I question much if he will care to
leave his own fireside."

"I was afraid you would be wet through, Jane,"
said Miss Dora, as she opened the door to her one
Sunday evening on her return from church. "How
is it your bonnet is not quite spoiled, for you had
no umbrella, and it rained so fast?"

"Why, miss, I did not know whatever I should
do. You know, miss, my sister Lizzie mostly

meets me and we sit together at church, and when
we came out and saw how it rained, she was fit to
cry at the thought of her new shawl being done for,
and she cried out loud enough for everybody to
hear, 'Oh! Jane,' she says, 'we shall be wet
through, what shall we do?' 'Why,' I said, 'come
home with me, to be sure, we ain't salt that we shall
melt;' and then a civil-spoken young man came
up, and said he saw we had no umbrella, and he
was hoping we would have his. You see, miss, he
wasn't anything but civil spoken, and so I said,
'Thank you,' and he brought me to the door and
is going Lizzie's way, and promised to see her
home too."

"Do you know his name, Jane?"

"No, miss, but I think he comes to church most
Sundays."

"Oh, very well," said Dora, "I am glad you did
not get wet. So now make haste, as mamma will
be glad of supper that she may go to bed early;
to-morrow morning is her morning, you know."

Twice during the week Mrs. Wilson was obliged
to leave home very early, having to give some
lessons at a distance. Jane was always up and
had everything in readiness for breakfast by seven
o'clock, and never allowed her mistress to leave the
house without seeing that she had her umbrella or

overshoes, or without paying her every attention she could think of. She did not admire a wet morning, but her voice was quite cheery if it was fine. " Such a nice morning, ma'am, the sun shines lovely ; " and the kindly tone of voice seemed to make the morning more beautiful to Mrs. Wilson, and the task before her lighter. So much can kindness and sympathy lighten labour.

Perhaps, in no way can we do so much to fulfil " the law of Christ " in bearing "one another's bur- dens," as by showing ready sympathy. In many cases it is all we can give, and surely it is wrong to withhold it because the gift seems so small, so much of the comfort of life depends on apparently *little* things. What can be *little* if it adds even an atom to the happiness of another ! Some people, wise in their own eyes, may be heard to say, " I keeps myself to myself, and neither meddles nor makes with my neighbours ; " meaning, in other words, that they are too selfish to interest them- selves in the joys or sorrows of others. Such people may be worldly wise, but as a rule are not loveable, and lose more than they gain ; for sym- pathy certainly blesses both giver and receiver.

The next Sunday evening the "civil young man " again escorted Jane home from church, and of course her young ladies joked her about her sweetheart, and asked her whether he was tall or short, and if she had discovered his name and what business he worked at.

Certainly he had contrived to convey a good deal of information during the short walk from church, for he had told her his name was William Matthews, he was twenty-five years of age, and worked at Mr. Sandars' foundry, where his father and grandfather had also worked all their lives. Jane allowed that he was not over good-looking, but "he was respectable and minded his church regular."

Mrs. Wilson, finding that it was a regular custom now for the young man to attend Jane home from church, told her she should like to see him and talk to him. Mrs. Wilson was not one of those mistresses who strictly forbid followers, as servants' lovers are usually called. She used to say, " I married myself, why should not my servant do the same? But as I hate deceit, I like to have all things fair and open, and to be satisfied that any young man looking after a servant of mine is respectable, and means to act fairly and honestly by her. I think it is a duty that mistresses owe their servants as members (for the time they are in their service) of the family."

So William Matthews was asked into the drawing-room, and at first looked a little shy and uncomfortable, but Mrs. Wilson's kind voice and pleasant manner soon set him tolerably at his ease. She told him she fancied he had a liking for Jane, and as she had conducted herself very well during the time she had lived in her service, she was anxious to know if he had the means to maintain a wife, and also if the master for whom he worked would speak well of him.

"Thank ye, ma'am, very kindly," replied William, "I'm earning a matter of eighteen shillings a week, and maybe I may get a rise. I never had an ill word with the master, and I've worked for him ever since I was thirteen years old, and I ain't no ways afeard of your asking him about me. You see, ma'am, a feller is lonesome without a wife to keep things tidy and make a place comfortable, so I says to myself, when I sees Jane coming regular to church, and minding the service so attentive like, and never staring about her, and looking so tidy and trim, ses I, that's the girl for my money; and please God we comes together, she shan't have cause to complain of taking me, for I'll do my best to make her a good husband."

"Indeed," said Mrs. Wilson, "I am very glad to hear you speak so honestly and in so straight-forward a manner. Jane is a good girl, and has

served me well, and though I shall be sorry to part
with her, I shall do so willingly, to give her to an
honest, upright man. She has done her duty to
me, and I doubt not she will make a good wife. I
suppose you will like to see her sometimes, so you
will be welcome to come here one evening in the
week; suppose we say every Wednesday, and I
shall expect that you will not stay later than ten
o'clock. Of course I shall make enquiries about
you, in justice to you and Jane; and now, good
night, if you like you may go downstairs this evening, I daresay you will find something to talk
about."

William accordingly took his departure, and did
find his way downstairs, where no doubt he and
Jane talked about many matters interesting to
themselves, but of which no record is left.

Mrs. Wilson knew something of Mr. Sandars,
William's master, and, therefore, had no difficulty
in making enquiries as to his character, and she
was glad to find the favourable impression he had
made on her was fully warranted.

Mr. Sandars considered him one of his most
promising hands. He knew him to be a good son
and an honest, steady fellow; he was very glad to
find he was likely to marry a sensible, steady girl,
for he had known so many instances, in his long

experience of workmen, in which men's lives had been ruined by marrying young girls who cared for nothing but being married, and having a house of their own. Working-men have not many opportunities of knowing much of the character of the girls they seek for wives ; they meet them generally on Sundays, their only leisure time, and a girl dressed out in her Sunday clothes is a very different looking being to the untidy woman she so often becomes in her own home.

Mr. Sandars was a kind and considerate master, and interested himself more than many in the welfare of his work-people. He often deplored the hasty manner in which some men jumped into matrimony, caught, perhaps, by a pretty face, and finding, to their cost, that a pretty face alone, without good principles, won't long keep a man's house comfortable or make the most of his wages ; and as men in general are not gifted with much patience, they are apt, and surely with some excuse, to turn from their own hearths and seek pleasure out of doors.

"I do not think," said Mr. Sandars, "that will be Matthews' way ; and I am very glad he proves himself, in this important matter, as sensible a fellow as I have taken him for." And the next time he met William, he told him of the enquiries

Mrs. Wilson had made, and how pleased he was to hear he was going to settle down with a girl who was so well spoken of by her mistress. "You must let me know when the affair comes off, and I shall let you have the day, so that you may have a holiday with your wife and your friends."

William touched his cap and thanked his master, who, as he afterwards told Jane, was a real gentleman, and no mistake.

Jane's courtship went on very smoothly, and she and William seemed very contented with each other's company, as indeed lovers generally are, though some do consider a tiff now and then as necessary. Lovers' quarrels are too much like playing with edged tools to be always advisable, beside the coming to is so awkward. Certainly, Jane did not always agree with William on every point, especially as regarded their marriage. Of course, he wanted to be married off-hand; what was the good of waiting? He wanted a wife, and he was sure a kind lady like Mrs. Wilson would not mind sparing her—had not Jane better speak to her at once?

"Why, William, how can you talk so! though, to be sure, you can't be expected to know missus's ways, and what would be convenient or not. Well, then, Christmas 'll come soon, and I can't think of leaving then ; what 'ud missus do with a new girl in the dark weather, one as did not know her ways ? She does get a bit of a holiday then, and so do the young ladies, and much of a holiday it would be to have a stupid to look after ; it would be sure to make Miss Ellen ill, and who would nurse her ? and missus is not strong. And then there's Miss Dora, why, she has got to look after her wedding things, and ain't much use in the house ; and Miss Mary, law ! she is after her books and her playing, so you must just wait, and I daresay it will do you good, you will be all the wiser. You see, you were a dear old stupid to think of my going just yet, so be a good patient boy, and then in the spring we'll see ; besides, I wouldn't go to any man's home without tidy clothes, and, bless you ! I've got lots to do yet."

Of course, William vowed she always looked tidy, and what more did he want ? To be sure, she must consider the missus and the young ladies ; he did not like waiting, but perhaps she was right, the missus was certainly very kind to them. In his heart he knew Jane's reasons were good and did her credit ; and though he might be vexed at delay, still he respected Jane more for her consideration for her mistress's comfort, and respect is a great strengthener of true love.

Jane did not tell him she had saved money, because, as she said to Mrs. Wilson, " It will come a nice little surprise, and there will be plenty of use for it, maybe, by and bye."

Mrs. Wilson was very glad Jane did not leave her in the depth of winter, for soon after Christmas the influenza became almost universal, and the whole family suffered from it, Mrs. and Miss Wilson the most severely.

Dora and Mary were ill first, and with them the disease was slight ; but Mrs. Wilson was very ill and confined to her bed, and a good deal of low fever hung about her, and made her very weak for some time. As to Ellen, she was always called Murad the Unlucky, as she had a knack of taking any illness in a severe form, and certainly this turn of influenza was no exception to her usual rule.

Jane escaped pretty well at first, but her turn came and she was obliged to lie by for a time ; she would not own she was ill, till she nearly fainted after carrying some arrowroot to Miss Wilson's room, when Dora exclaimed—

" There, Jane, I told you how it would be. Why did you not wait for me to fetch that ? Now you just come with me, and go to bed at once. I am quite strong now, and I shan't let you be nurse any longer."

C

" Please, miss, I must go and look after the beef-
tea that is on the fire, and then if you could
manage a little bit I will lie down. I shall soon
be better."

" I believe I am quite equal to beef-tea ; at any
rate, I mean to be, and you are not to be found in
the kitchen without my leave, so be off to bed, and
I will go and get the warming pan and make you
comfortable ; and you, Ellen, drink your arrowroot
like a lady while I am gone."

Jenny faintly protested against giving so much
trouble, but was obliged to submit, for in truth she
could hardly stand.

William was in great distress when he found
Jane was laid by ; but Dora consoled him somewhat by giving him a few little commissions to
execute for her out of doors, and getting him to
fill coal-scuttles and carry them upstairs. In those
days, when so many were ill, it was extremely
difficult to get a charwoman, and particularly in
places where they were seldom wanted. Jane
never would agree to have help if she could pos-
sibly do without, she " Couldn't abide them char-
women," as she used to say ; " I'd rather do the
work twice over than have that Mrs. Norris. How
she could ever work and stuff herself at the rate
she did, used to puzzle me ; and to see her drink

tea! six cups I've seen her have, and want another!
but I'd up and empty out the tea leaves for fear
she'd be ill."

The race may have improved since those days,
but a London-bred charwoman, thirty years ago,
was not generally a pleasant specimen of woman-
kind.

William's services were really valuable, and he
looked in every evening to see what he could do,
generally bringing some trifle in the shape of
oranges or a cake for Jane, for which she called
him a goose, but was, nevertheless, very gratified.
She did her best to get well by obeying the doctor's
orders, and taking the medicine and good things
that were considered proper for her. Her mistress
had not to say of her, as many have, that servants
are so tiresome to nurse, because they are so fan-
ciful and will not believe that others know what is
good for them better than they do themselves.

Miss Wilson was getting much better, and looking forward to going to a friend's for change of
air. Mrs. Wilson was able to begin her teaching
again. Dora and Mary had a busy time of it, but
were rather proud of their work, and told Jane she
would not find everything topsy-turvy, as they
knew she expected. "And you may go down to
tea to-night," said Dora, "and perhaps you may
have company."

So she had, for there was William, looking very red in the face with the effort of toasting a muffin he had brought for her tea, and which Jane said was very good; and though one side was over-done and the other nearly white, she would not have hurt his feelings for the world by saying so. They had a very pleasant meal, and altogether Jane looked so little tired on going to bed, that Dora told her she was half jealous, for she looked brighter and better, after sitting in William's company for two hours than with a whole week of her nursing.

"Oh, Miss Dora! William and me have been talking of your goodness to me, and he says how pleased he was to do anything for such a young lady who speaks so pleasant; and, indeed, miss, I can't think how you and Miss Mary have kept everything so tidy in the kitchen; and now I hope, please God, I shan't give you any more trouble."

"Well, I hope you won't," replied Dora, "for we have had a long nursing bout; but we must all feel very grateful to our Father in Heaven that we are all spared, and so far restored to health, while so many have been cut off. Shall I read you one of my favourite psalms?"

"Oh, if you please, miss; I do so love to hear you read."

So Dora read the 91st Psalm, and after talking of the comfort God's promises are to all, retired to rest very glad at heart that her labours had been so successful, under God's blessing. She had, too, cause for especial thankfulness that Mr. Lee had entirely escaped the prevailing epidemic.

The quiet little household resumed its usual uneventful course, and when the early spring days began to brighten the sky, Mrs. Wilson talked the matter over with her girls, and they agreed that it would be but right to remind Jane that they were willing to keep their promise of releasing her and providing themselves with another help. Jane said she was quite willing to wait till her mistress met with some one likely to suit her; but she and William had been talking of the Easter week being a good time to be married in, and his master had raised his wages to a pound a week, and there were some rooms to let in a street not far from the foundry that would just suit them.

So Mrs. Wilson made enquiries, and was fortunate to meet with a girl who seemed likely to suit her. Jane worked early and late to leave everything in apple-pie order, and gave the new servant many instructions about various domestic arrangements, and how "missus never eat any upper crust, and Miss Ellen could not eat her eggs boiled hard,"

&c. She hovered about Miss Ellen, and lingered
the last evening as if she could not bear to leave,
till at last Mrs. Wilson was obliged to say,

"Now, Jane, child, you really must go. I shan't
say much to you to-night; but, remember, I shall
always be glad to see you. If troubles should
come, as they do to all, come to me, and if I can
help you, you may be sure I will. Do your duty
to your husband as faithfully as you have done to
me, and you will have the comfort of a good con-
science. And now I must give you my present,"
and she produced a family Bible : " I give it with an
earnest prayer that you and your husband will seek
to guide your steps by its precepts. Make a
practice of at least finishing the day by reading a
chapter. You will find I have put a mark in the
beautiful chapter about wives at the end of the
Proverbs. The verses I have put a double mark
to I would advise you to learn by heart. And
now, good bye, God bless you ! "

Jane was quite overcome by Mrs. Wilson's kindness ; and after shaking hands with her and her
young ladies, she departed, carrying her precious
book, which she resolved should occupy the place
of honour in her new home.

The sun shone brightly on Jane's wedding morning, and she was astir betimes, as the ceremony

was to be at an early hour to allow of a long day in the country. She knelt by her bedside and prayed earnestly to Him whose ears are ever open to those who seek Him, that He would enable her to serve Him and to do her duty in the station to which He had called her. She then read the text Miss Wilson had written out for her,—" Let us run with patience the race set before us, looking unto Jesus, the author and finisher of our faith." God has been very good to me, thought Jane, and I do hope I shall be a good wife, at least, I'll try. The text says, "looking to Jesus," and that means He will help me. I must try and remember that " The Lord is my strength and my salvation."

Jane dressed herself in her neat new dress, a present from her young ladies, her sister had a holiday for the day, and they set off together for the church from the friend's house where she had stayed for the night. William and a friend, to act as father, met them at the church door ; and after the ceremony, which was felt to be a solemn service by both, they left the church, arm in arm, as man and wife.

William said he meant to make the most of his wedding day, so to do the thing in good style he had hired a nice tax cart, which his friend could drive, and the whole party would go and spend the

day in Epping Forest. And a very pleasant day
they had. Perhaps few people enjoy the country
so thoroughly as Londoners do ; the change is so
complete from the incessant noise and bustle to the
delicious quiet of green fields. The fresh air, free
from dust and smoke, is so exhilarating that no
wonder the spirits rise, and care, dull care, seems
left behind.

The wedding party were thorough cockneys, and
had very rarely enjoyed a day in the country, for
this was before the days of railroads. Their enjoy-
ment of sauntering through the picturesque nooks
of the Forest was intense, and was not lessened
by a good dinner, for, as William said, he would
have a good dinner that day anyways. There was
plenty of laughter and merriment, William advising
his friend to follow his example, and his friend
looking at Lizzie thought perhaps he might if he
could get anyone to have him. Whereat that
young woman blushed and laughed, and they all
laughed and were very happy, till it was pronounced to be time to put the horse to and get
homewards.

It was a lovely evening, and its calm beauty
sank into their hearts, making them happy and
peaceful, they scarcely knew why ; only as Jane
sat with her hand clasped in her husband's she had

a sense of rest and a fulness of content she never forgot. They set Lizzie down at her mistress's door, with a promise from her to come and see them the next Sunday, and then William took his wife to her own home.

PART THE SECOND.

THE WIFE AND MOTHER.

PART THE SECOND.

THE WIFE AND MOTHER.

JANE found plenty of occupation at first in her new home, which consisted of two rooms in a small house in one of the narrow streets leading from Chiswell Street. It was a handy locality for William, which was its chief recommendation; otherwise it was a dull situation, or only enlivened by sights and sounds that were not cheering. Jane made her own small rooms look bright and cheerful, as cleanliness and neatness will do for even the poorest dwelling. But when she had arranged everything to her satisfaction, and seen that her husband's clothes were in perfect repair, she began to find she had a good deal of time hanging heavy on her hands. Her husband went to his work at six o'clock, and as to wasting her own time in bed she never thought of it. Breakfast time at eight o'clock found the household work considerably advanced, so that when the

breakfast things were put away, and her preparations made for dinner, with perhaps a little
marketing, there was nothing to do.

Young wives generally feel this want of occupation, more especially when they have been accustomed to an active life. Too many misuse this
time terribly and lay the foundation of indolent
habits, that have sad effects in future years. A
thoughtless woman will gossip with her neighbours
and learn to dawdle in a very short time, and bad
habits are much more easily learned than they are
easy to lay aside. There is an old Swedish proverb
that " Idleness is the devil's cushion."

Now, cushions are very comfortable things in
their way, but young healthy people do not want
cushions, and better not begin to use them. It is
not a matter of astonishment that a young girl
used all her life to hard work should feel it a great
thing to be mistress of her own time, free to manage
her own house just as she pleases; it is very natural,
and there is nothing wrong in it, only she should
remember in time to guard against falling into lazy
ways.

Jane Matthews could not be idle ; it was not in
her nature, and she was not given to gossiping.
She hardly knew what it was that made the time
seem so long between meals, they were generally

ready before William came home, for she had no
clock to tell her the exact time, which was very
inconvenient. So she propounded some of her
trouble to William ; of course she had told him she
had saved money, though she had let him buy the
furniture, knowing, as she said, that her savings
would come in handy some time.

Well, she proposed to buy a clock, to which he
willingly agreed, so he drew £4 out of the Savings'
Bank, which was just half she had. A large new
clock was out of the question, but after some search
a second-hand one was found for £3 10s., and with
the remaining ten shillings Jane bought some little
household things she found necessary.

Miss Wilson and Dora had been to see her, and
reported to mamma how comfortable she seemed,
and they had waited to see William come in to tea
in order to congratulate him, and he seemed very
proud and happy.

" Jenny said she should soon come and see you,
mamma, as she wants some advice. I asked her,"
continued Ellen, " what she did with herself while
William was at work, and she said the only trouble
she had was, the days were so long."

" I daresay she won't complain of that long,"
replied her mamma ; " she will find occupation
soon enough, though now I daresay she may find
time hang rather heavily on her hands."

Jane soon found her way to Finsbury on an afternoon she knew she was likely to find Mrs. Wilson at home.

"Well, Jenny," said Miss Mary, "here you come at last, looking just the same; does she not, mamma?"

"I should hope so," replied her mamma, "I do not like my friends to change. I am glad to see you like your old self, and hope you are quite comfortably settled."

"Thank'e, ma'am, I am very well and happy, and glad to see you looking so well; and William sends his duty to you and the young ladies."

"Well, I hope he has not repented yet of getting married."

"I do not think he does, ma'am," said Jane, blushing.

"Ah, it's early days yet," said Miss Mary, "and he has not found out yet what a dragon you can be; but now, show me your wedding ring, you keep it so covered up."

"It is a good thick one," said Mrs. Wilson, as Jane exhibited her hand, "and I hope you will live to wear it out."

"Are you not afraid of washing it off?" said Mary, "I think I should be."

"It was rather strange the first day or two,"

replied Jane, "but I'm quite used to it now. I've been married three weeks, you know."

" Yes, I remember, and you ought to have been here before ; but I must go now, for I am hard at work and cannot spare time for gossiping, even with Mrs. Matthews—really it sounds quite grand !" and off ran Mary, leaving Jane alone with Mrs. Wilson.

After making enquiries for Miss Wilson and Miss Dora, Jane begged Mrs. Wilson, as a favour, to give her some work to do.

" Well, Jane, I would gladly give you some, but you know we always do the work that would be suitable for you ourselves, principally because we cannot afford to pay for putting plain work out."

" Oh ! ma'am," said Jane, " I do not want to be paid ; I want some work to fill up my time."

" That would not be fair to you, Jane," replied Mrs. Wilson, "though I quite believe it would give you pleasure to do something for us."

" Indeed it would, ma'am, for you are the best friend I ever had ; and you know, ma'am, I could do some needlework, for you always have so much to do in other ways."

" That is true," replied Mrs. Wilson, "but you must remember that time is money, and I have no more right to your time than I have to your money.

I should not like always to deprive you of the pleasure of doing any little things for me or any other friend, but to give you work to do for me regularly would not be right for either of us. My idea is, that you should try and get work from some warehouse—that is a more independent way, and would suit you better than working for friends. There are a good many wholesale warehouses in your neighbourhood, I know, and you would have but little difficulty in getting some work that would employ your leisure time. The pay is not high probably, but it would be certain, and you would find the money useful some day. Don't spend your earnings, as your husband's wages ought to be quite enough ; but lay them by for a future day, and you may depend upon it they will be very useful. You asked my advice, and I give you the best I can."

" I'm sure, ma'am, you are very good," said Jane, "and I'll try and do as you tell me, only if you do want any little odd job done at any time, do let me do it for you."

" Oh, I daresay I shall find something for you, and I should not wonder if you will want to come and help when Miss Dora is married."

" Oh ! ma'am, is the time settled ? " asked Jane.

" The day is not fixed," replied Mrs. Wilson,

" but I expect we shall lose her in July. Mr. Lee does not like waiting any longer, he says he wants a housekeeper."

" Well, ma'am, I don't wonder ; for men are poor things by themselves."

" Yes," said Mrs. Wilson, " housekeeping is woman's work, and very important work too ; you could not do your husband's work, and it is not to be expected he should do yours."

" That's true, ma'am, thank you for talking to me, and I'll try and get some work to-morrow."

" Well, talk to your husband about it."

" Oh, ma'am, he'll be sure to say it's all right," said Jane, " if you bid me do anything. He thinks you know everything."

" Not quite," replied Mrs. Wilson, smiling at William's opinion of her abilities ; " but I have lived a little longer in the world than you, and used my brains. And now, good bye for to-day, I shall be glad to know how you get on ; and do not forget to take some exercise, it will not do for you to sit still all day, you have not been used to it, and nothing will recompense you for loss of health ; you should get your husband out for a walk some of these nice evenings, you would both be all the better for it."

" Well, old woman, what did the missus say to

you?" asked William, as they sat over their tea, which Jane had got home in time to get ready.

"Oh, missus is quite well, and asked me how I got on at home; and Miss Mary wanted to know whether you were tired of me yet," replied Jane.

"Oh, did she? Well, I think I can put up with you a bit longer," said William; "you fit into the place here pretty tidy like. What do you think of a bit of a turn this nice evening?"

"Why, it would be just the thing I should like," said Jane.

"That's your sort," said William, "and I'll tidy up a bit, and we'll go on London Bridge and see the boats come in."

On their way to the Bridge, Jane told her husband how she meant to get some work the next day. He could not see she could want more to do; there was the dinner to cook, and his buttons to sew on, besides lots of fallals women wore which must take a heap of time to do. Jane laughed and said now she had sewed all his buttons on she did not think they would come off in a hurry, and it was only his nonsense about women's fallals, she hadn't many.

"Oh, very well, do as you like, if you and the missus says it's right, I'm agreeable."

So that matter was settled, and they enjoyed

their walk, finding the fresh air from the water and the amusement of watching the passengers land from the steamboats very pleasant. Many an evening they spent thus, to the great benefit of their health.

Jane had no difficulty in getting work, and perhaps my readers may like to know what she found to do. It must be remembered that fashions have altered very much in thirty years, and also that in those days there were no sewing machines. For many years a great deal of blond edging, run on to plain blond, was universally worn for caps, quilled fully round the face. An immense quantity was worn, as it did not keep clean long and was done for when dirty. Running on the edging was a simple kind of work, requiring only expedition and cleanliness; the pay was therefore, of course, small, about one penny for every dozen yards. Jane could, without neglecting any of her own affairs, run a good many dozen yards in the course of a week, and at the end of a few months had laid by a nice little sum. It must not be supposed that Jane was too strongly inclined to save, no one was more ready to give, both time and money, when really needed; but if she had not been careful she would not have had anything in her power to give when it was wanted.

"Did you get your breakfast all right, Will?" enquired Jane, as she greeted her husband at dinner time, one day.

"Yes, pretty well, considering," said William; "though I expect I left the things in a pretty mess. And how did the wedding go off, Jenny? I would ha' run round to the church to have had a look at Miss Dora; but I was peckish and wanted my breakfast, that's the truth, and I couldn't spare the time."

"Oh, she looked just beautiful, not fine, you know," said Jane, "but so nice; and Mr. Lee looked quite the gentleman, and he said he liked to see me there, it was like old times. You know the wedding was very early, so we laid the breakfast last night, and very pretty it looked with the cake in the middle of the table; and I've got a bit for you. Miss Dora said you were to be sure and come and drink her health. Missus was very quiet, I don't think she half likes parting with Miss Dora, though she looked very proud of her son-in-law. They set off as soon as they had done breakfast, as they had a long way to go; I just stayed to help Ann to put away the things while Miss Wilson packed up Miss Dora's wedding dress and things, and then I came home. Missus made me bring some fowl and ham home with me, so we shall have quite a grand dinner."

"And I know I've got good sauce for it, so wishing them as happy as we be, I'm ready to handle my knife and fork—jolly good it looks too," remarked William, sitting down to table.

Some months passed away very quietly and happily. William had a few little crooks in his temper, as most people have ; and, had Jane been so disposed, she could have got up a few domestic broils as easily as anyone. But she was a wise little woman in her way, and learned to hold her tongue when necessary ; as she used to say,

" Law, it takes two to make a quarrel, and I ain't going to be one. What's the use of contradicting him ? Will's a good fellow, and his bits of temper don't last."

She had not studied her chapter of Proverbs in vain, " In her mouth was the law of kindness," and truly, " the heart of her husband did safely trust in her." Oh that women would learn the use of silence ! Who was ever heard to regret having kept silence ? and how many have lived to rue the day they answered railing with railing !

Mrs. Matthews was a proud woman when she carried her baby boy to show him to Mrs. Wilson. She was, therefore, rather vexed to find Mrs. Wilson was out and only Miss Mary at home.

"Well, Jenny," said Mary, "I am very glad to see you out again ; and now let me see the baby. I am rather curious about babies, and do not think I ever saw one quite so young. Dear me ! what a funny little morsel it is, so soft and warm."

"He is rather small, miss, but very good, and sleeps so well at night," said Jane, looking fondly at the "little morsel," as Mary called him, and who just then made such a comical face that she laughed outright. "It was only the wind, miss ; there, hush, baby, hush ! "

"Why," said Mary, "I should think you had been nursing all your life, you do it so handily."

"Sure, miss, it seems to come natural like, only I was very trembly when I dressed him first."

"Well, let me have him a bit," said Mary, "and you fetch the parcel that is on the side table, Dora left it for you when she was here last. I was to give it to you with her love."

Jane put the baby into Miss Mary's arms, where, like a model child, he went comfortably to sleep ; and Jane opened her parcel, and in it found a pretty white frock for the baby.

"Oh ! what a beauty !" exclaimed Jane, "and so nicely made too ; how kind it was of Miss Dora to think of my baby—I beg her pardon, I mean Mrs. Lee."

"Yes," said Mary, "she hoped it would be in time for the christening. Have you thought of a name?"

"It's to be next Sunday, miss. I wanted to call him William, after his father; but he said he didn't think that would do, as by and bye, people would be for calling them 'old Will' and 'young Will,' and for his part he didn't fancy to be called old anything yet awhile. So then we thought of George being a good sounding name. Don't you think it is, miss?"

"Oh, very nice indeed," replied Mary; "but here comes Ellen, and she will give you her opinion."

Jane was delighted to see Miss Wilson, and the baby had to be exhibited again, and show the pretty pink toes, and all the interesting little details of babyhood, so very dear to mothers, young mothers especially. Miss Wilson quite approved the name of George, which she observed was a name fit for a true Briton, as she hoped he would be all his life.

"And I suppose William is very fond of it," continued she. "Does he do much nursing?"

"Well, not much yet, miss; he calls him 'the young shaver," and likes to see him on my lap, but he is half afraid to handle him for fear of letting him fall."

" Ah!" said Miss Wilson, " he will get his hand
in by the time you have another. Mamma will be
sorry to have missed you, but she is spending the
evening with Mrs. Lee. Mary, you ought to have
had your tea and not waited for me, I am so much
later than I expected. Jane, you must be quite
famished."

" Indeed, miss, I must go ; William will be wondering what is become of me."

" Well, never mind his wondering for once, Jane,"
said Miss Wilson ; " you will be fainting by the
way for want of something to eat, and you do not
look very strong yet. Of course William knows
where you are, and will come after you, if it is
only to see that we have not quite eaten the baby
up."

Jane smiled and looked quite happy in her old
quarters; and soon after tea, as Miss Wilson antici-
pated, her husband made his appearance, apolo-
gizing for coming with the excuse, that he thought,
maybe, Jane would be tired with carrying the
young 'un so far the first time.

Miss Wilson carried the baby downstairs, and
told his father he had been quite a pattern baby,
which gratified him greatly. She told Jane she
should be sure and remember her next Sunday,
and she hoped baby would grow up to be a blessing
to her and his father.

Jane had no reason to complain of having nothing to do, after the birth of her baby, for he was a delicate child, always taking cold and cutting his teeth with difficulty. When in the course of a year and a half another baby made its appearance, it may be guessed her hands were fully occupied. Still she was never so busy but she could find time to help a neighbour in distress. It was well known in her immediate neighbourhood that if any one was ill, or wanted a child minded, or a bit of washing done, that Mrs. Matthews was the one to apply to, and rarely did any one apply in vain.

However she might be occupied for her children or a neighbour, she never neglected her husband, his comfort was her first care ; she could shift the little ones, she used to say, but the father ought to have his meals regular and comfortable, she had no notion of making the children first and father second. Consequently, as his home looked pleasant, his wife with a cheerful face, and the children taught to look for "father," he had far more inducements to stay at home than to go loitering about by himself.

Jane was always kind and hospitable to anyone of his fellow-workmen he liked to bring home with him for a chat, and she would join in the talk, while she sat at her work, in a cheerful way she

had, that made an evening so spent very pleasant
Some people in her circumstances might say they
could not afford to have company at home, but she
would maintain that a man must have some amusement, and if he went from home he would be sure
to spend something, and she thought it was nicer
that he should have a little pleasure by his own
fireside.

Jane did not now see quite so much of her mistress and her family as she used to do, for they had
removed to a greater distance. A great sorrow
had fallen upon them in the death of the youngest,
Miss Mary. When Jane called soon after and
found Mrs. Lee and her baby son staying on a
visit, she could hardly notice the child, so much
was she overcome by the loss of its aunt.

"To think she did not see it, poor little dear!"
said Jane to her husband, on her return home;
"and poor missus looks so sad, and the place did
not seem a bit like it used to. Miss Ellen looked
very poorly, though she tried to speak as cheerful
as she could for the missus' sake. She was never
a one to think of herself; and she talked to
Georgy, and said what a man he had grown, and
how she hoped he would grow up a good boy;
and what a comfort it was to them, now she was
gone, to know that dear Miss Mary must be so

happy, because she had been a good daughter and trusted to her Saviour. I'm sure, thinking of her will make me try more and more to make my boys good boys—God bless 'em! it would be very hard to part with 'em."

Troubles were coming on Jenny that taxed her strength and courage considerably. Trade was very bad all over England, and in many manufactories wages were being reduced; the harvest had been a scanty one, consequently bread was dear, so that any reduction in wages was felt to be a very great hardship. Grumbling and discontent were very rife, and working-men began to talk of striking for increased pay, not considering that masters would have been glad enough to pay them better if trade allowed them to do so. It may be remembered that Mr. Sandars, William Matthews' master, was a kind man, but he was obliged to submit to the pressure of the times, and calling his men together, he told them that he was compelled to reduce their wages. He hoped it would not be for long, but as it was he could not help himself.

William and several others were willing to work on, knowing the master would not have come to such a resolution had it been possible to avoid it; and as William said, "Half a loaf was better than no bread." But there were two or three men amongst them, blustering fellows, more inclined to talk than work, and they vowed that not another stroke of work should be done in the foundry till the master was made to pay the same wages as formerly. By dint of loud talk they gained over the weaker ones, and having the greater number on their side they were able to dictate to the rest. So a strike was the consequence, and William was thrown out of work. To be sure, he was better off than some, for there were Jane's savings to fall back upon for a time; but when it is all going out and nothing coming in, money soon vanishes. Jane did all she could to make things last; and a little money in her hands went further than it did with many; but with all her care and forethought, they got behindhand with the rent.

The strike ended at last, having continued fourteen weeks, and William went to work again. He had been induced by necessity to apply to a loan office for £5 to be repaid with interest at a year's end. It had been rather against Jane's wish that he had borrowed money at all; but when once done, she did not worry him with regrets.

"What's done can't be helped," she would say, "and I must make the best of it."

Her two boys, George and James, were two nice children, inheriting a fair share of their mother's

even temper, but not very robust in health.   She
made them obedient, and as she was always truthful with them, they trusted her implicitly—anything
mother said was relied on in perfect good faith.
They were small of their age, as so many London
children are.   When one was about five and the
other three and a half, a little sister was added to
the family, to the great delight of the boys, who,
unlike a good many children, thought a new baby
was a precious thing.   Jane was not often very
angry; when she was, it was a thing to be remembered ; and she was very indignant when she heard
a neighbour tell George, shortly before his sister's
birth, that "His nose would soon be put out of
joint." It was an expression common enough and
often repeated, simply because it is a saying ; but
it was one that Jenny could not hear with patience.

"Stop," she said, "don't put such a thought into
the boy's head. God tells little children to love
one another, and is that the way to do it when you
try to make them jealous?"

"Oh, Mrs. Matthews, I didn't mean anything ;
it was only my nonsense," said Mrs. Jones.

"Maybe you didn't," replied Jane, "but nonsense
of that sort does a deal of mischief, and a child
can't tell but what it's true, and I don't want my
children to hate one another."

"Law!" said Mrs. Jones, "I begs your pardon, I never thought of it like that; as you say, it's stupid, but then people don't think."

"No, and more's the pity," replied her friend; "a deal of mischief just comes out of not thinking."

The time was drawing near when the borrowed £5 must be repaid, and Matthews had not been able to save anything like enough to meet the claim. Poor fellow! it was hard on an honest man who had the will to pay. To be in debt was quite new to him, and he did not know anyone he could ask to help him, even if he could have screwed up courage enough to ask. So he was at his wit's end, and naturally consoled his wife, as the manner of man is, with anticipations of ruin, and being sent to gaol, and she and the children to the workhouse, and other agreeable doings. Jane did her best to keep his spirits up, and told him that they had done their best, and she was sure help would come somehow. She had great faith in the silver lining to the darkest cloud, and knew too, in this case, that she had excellent grounds for her faith.

"To think of your coming to the workhouse, Jenny, and breaking up the home. I shan't be fit to look the children in the face again," almost sobbed William, after walking up and down the room some time.

"Nonsense, old man," said Jenny, "I haven't been quite idle all this time—look here!" and she went to a cupboard where, out of an old teapot, she produced five sovereigns. "There, you won't get sent to gaol this time, and I ain't going to the workhouse, thank God. Don't be afraid, it's all honestly come by, so go and make a free man of yourself, once more."

Matthews could hardly believe his own eyes.

"But where did you get it?" he asked; "I can't make it out."

"Why, you see, Will," said his wife, "I knowed you'd want it, and I got work to do, and I've saved every penny I could anyways do without, and then I do think God has helped me especial."

"Well, you are a jewel of an old woman; give us a kiss and I'll go and pay these yellow boys back again, and come back and we'll have a cosy evening."

Mrs. Matthews soon after paid Mrs. Wilson a visit, she had not seen her for a long time, as she could not well spare the time. Mrs. Wilson made many enquiries about her affairs, and Jane told her about the borrowed money, and what a way Will was in, and how she had saved up the necessary sum.

"But why did you not tell him," enquired her friend, "what you were doing?"

"Well, ma'am, you see, I thought," replied Jane, "it was but fair he should have some of the worry as well as me; and I don't think after this he will be in a hurry to go to a loan office again."

After Jane was gone Mrs. Wilson was talking the matter over with her daughter, and she observed,

"Who would think, to look at that little woman, so plain and insignificant as she is in appearance, that she had such a brave spirit. I call her a heroine; and among all the people I know, and my acquaintance with life is not small, there is no one I more highly respect than Jane Matthews."

"Yes, indeed," said Miss Wilson, "I quite agree with you, and such a frail little body as she is too. She is not looking well, and no wonder, with all the hard work she has had lately. I was glad to hear her say she intended to move in March, for that neighbourhood she lives in is very close and confined. She never was strong herself, and the children do not seem healthy. I wish I could send them all for a month to the sea-side."

"I daresay you do, my dear," replied Mrs. Wilson, "and so should I; but you know, if 'wishes were horses, beggars would ride,' and I suppose that would hardly be tolerated now-a-days. She will not lose her reward, that is one blessing. Poor as her lot seems to us to be here, how many of the

E

rich would be glad to change places with her hereafter, for truly she has been faithful with little."

As soon as Jane was able to turn herself round, as she expressed it, and things began to look a little brighter, she set about looking for a house. It was her idea to give up lodgings, have a house of her own, and get a couple of men to board and lodge, that would help pay the rent. William was rather afraid of such an undertaking, but he had had so much cause to trust his wife that he agreed to try it, and do his best to get two tidy fellows as lodgers.

"I heard Dick Styles growling at the way his landlady put upon him the other day," said William, "and I've a notion he'd jump at the offer, so get a berth and I'll put the question; he's a steady chap enough, and when one's found I daresay we shall start another, there ain't no fear of their being comfortable."

Finding a house to suit was not altogether an easy matter; it was not what was pretty outside, but what was convenient inside that Jane looked after. At last one was found, that had as many conveniences as could be expected for the rent she could afford, in a clean paved court, a quiet place, such as there are in many parts of the city. It required a good deal of management to make the furniture stretch over a larger space, and some new things were necessities. But Jane was a capital hand at a bargain, and bore in mind her mistress' old precept, "Never buy anything only because it is cheap."

William was a handy man in a house, and could put up shelves, and do many odd jobs that tend so much to make a home convenient and tidy. Many an old bit of furniture she picked up at the broker's for an old song, because it was out of repair in sundry ways, was made quite useful and neat by dint of mending and patching.

Miss Wilson paid her a visit when she was settled, and was highly amused with some of her arrangements, and by the history of some of her new acquisitions, which she related in the quaint way that was habitual to her. Things had been bought expressly for use, but they seemed quite at home, and to fit into their places in a wonderfully comfortable way, and imparted a cosy look that is often deficient in places of far greater pretensions.

"You do look quite settled indeed," said Miss Wilson ; "and have you any lodgers yet ?"

"Yes, miss," replied Jane, "two very tidy young men ; they have the back bedroom and they have their meals with us."

"But you must have a good deal more to do?" said Miss Wilson.

"Yes, indeed, miss, what with one thing and another, and their bit of washing too, but it all comes into the day's work," said Jane. "Please, miss, now you are here, will you write baby's name in the Bible? You've done the rest, and I couldn't bear no one to write in it after you."

"Certainly," replied Miss Wilson. "What is the name? I quite forget."

"Oh, we called her after you, miss—Ellen, if you please: William thinks it's the prettiest name for a girl."

"What! better than Jane?" asked Miss Wilson.

"Oh, a deal, miss," replied Jane; "he likes it well enough, he says, because it's mine, but it ain't pretty; so I says I ain't pretty nor never was, so we just match, my name and me. Baby favours her father, don't you think so, miss?"

"Well, I think she does, rather," said Miss Wilson; "she has more colour in her cheeks than the boys, and her eyes are like her father's; but now I must write the name. I am glad to see the book looks as if it was used and not kept only for show."

"We keep that for Sunday afternoons," said Jane; "William will read me a chapter, and you can't think how quiet the little 'uns sit, one on each side of him, and listen so attentive; and are so proud to say a bit of a hymn to him. It's my bit of quiet in the week ; I don't think I could get on without my Sunday afternoon and church in the evening. I do try to go in the morning, but I can't manage it always."

"I should hardly think you could," said Miss Wilson ; "if we do what we can we know we are obeying our Lord and Master, who is willing to accept even our imperfect service, if offered with a faithful and loving heart. There, I've written my namesake's name, so good-bye, little one ; grow up a good woman like your mother. Good bye, Jenny, come and see us when you have time : I think I have some stuff that will make baby a frock."

The years that had passed away had left their traces on Jane Matthews, as they do on all. She had become stouter and more matronly-looking, and was the mother of four children ; another girl having been added to her family. Her husband continued to work at the foundry, and hoped in time to get one of his boys there also. In the meantime he tried hard to give them as much schooling as he could, and he would not let them have anything to do with the idle, ill-behaved lads that abound everywhere.

" I've worked hard all my time," he would say,

"and my boys must too; and they'd find it precious hard to buckle to, if they got a taste for loafing about now."

But he was not harsh, and was generally ready to enter into any of their little plans of play; so they were not at all afraid of him, though they knew he would be obeyed. Their mother had never used any such threat, as "I'll tell father;" so they looked upon father and mother as their friends, as indeed parents ought to be to their children, and, thank God, are in many cases. Where they are not, who is to blame? Surely the parents, whose duty it is to teach their children *obedience* from their very earliest days. It is not a lesson that can, with any safety, be put off; for as the poet says,

"Just as the twig is bent the tree's inclined."

One day Mrs. Matthews, being busy, sent her little girl Ellen (Nelly she was generally called) to the grocer's for some rice and sugar, and gave her a shilling to pay for them, and was surprised to see her return very quickly, empty-handed.

"Well, Nelly, where's the rice? I want it, the pudding won't be done for dinner," said her mother.

"I haven't got it," said the child; "the woman

you sent told me as you had said she was to go, and you wanted me."

"What woman, child? I never sent any woman, you may be sure. Where's the shilling?" said her mother.

"Oh! I gave her that to buy the things for you," answered the child.

"How could you be so simple?" exclaimed Jane.

"Well, but, mother," said Nelly, innocently, "she said you told me to give it her, and so I did."

"You little goose! don't you go to believe what people says to you in the streets," said her mother. "You'll get no pudding for dinner, and I must give you a whipping to make you remember another time. I was sorry enough to do it," said Jane to her husband, after explaining why his dinner was rather short; "but, you know, she don't hear lies at home, and the little puss takes everything for gospel that's said to her, and that won't do out of doors, you know. Here, Nelly, come and kiss father; and you won't hearken to naughty people, who tell lies, again in the streets, will you? Mother can't afford to lose shillings."

Nelly was a very truthful child, and couldn't understand why she was whipped because the naughty woman took her money; but the lesson was not lost on her, and no one ever had the oppor-

tunity of robbing her again.   As a little treat, after
the distress Nelly had been in, her mother promised
to take her and Polly, the little one, to see her old
friend, Mrs. Wilson, that afternoon.

The children were greatly delighted, as the way
to that lady's house was past a great number of
beautiful shops ; and they knew Miss Wilson generally had some pretty things to show them, and
there were such grand pictures on the walls.   The
dinner things were soon cleared with the help of
the little ones, and they set off, and fortunately
found Mrs. Wilson and Miss Ellen at home.   Many
mutual enquiries were made, and Jane was telling
how she had brought the children with her for a
great treat, when the door opened and a curly-
headed little girl peeped in, and was just running
off when Miss Wilson said,

"Come here, Nelly, I want you."

The little one ran up to her, and turning shyly
round, looked up at Jane.

"Oh," said Jane, "that must be your little niece,
miss ; how like she is to Miss Dora."

"There, go and shake hands," said her aunt ;
"that is a very old friend of mamma's, and these
are her little girls."

After shaking hands and giving Jane a kiss, that
quite won her heart, Miss Wilson suggested to

Nelly to take the little ones with her and show them her playthings. Nothing loth, the little ones started off together, and were duly introduced to dolly and a wonderful doll's house.

"What a pretty little thing she is!" said Jane, after the children had left the room. "I hope Mrs. Lee is quite well."

"No, indeed," replied Mrs. Wilson, "I went to see her this summer, and found her in a very weak state of health, quite unfit to have children about her, so I brought Nelly home with me, and we shall keep her till her mamma is stronger. She is a good child and quite a companion for her aunt. And now, Jenny, give an account of yourself. How are you getting on at home? With your lodgers and your children you do not find time hang so heavily on your hands as it used to do."

"I'm mostly busy enough," said Jane, "but I do a bit of work at odd times for the shops, or a bit of washing. It takes a deal to keep the house, and what with the schooling, and one thing and another, it ain't easy to make both ends meet; but, thank God! we ain't in debt."

"And how is William?" asked Mrs. Wilson, "I suppose he continues to think you the best wife in London."

"He is pretty well, ma'am," replied Jane. "We

don't often fall out, but he did try a bit of jealousy though."

"William jealous!" exclaimed Miss Wilson; "how could that come to pass, and what naughty deed had you been doing of all people in the world?"

"Why, you see, ma'am," answered Jane, "there's a neighbour of ours, a Mrs. Barker; and, poor soul, she had a very bad confinement, and no one much to see to her, so of course I couldn't but go and do what I could for the poor thing; I did some washing for her and kept the children out of her way. They had not lived there long, and Will didn't know much of them; not that he'd mind my doing anything for any poor sick body. After she got better her husband looked in one evening to thank me for helping his wife, which was very civil, you know, ma'am. William had just come in to tea, and as it was all ready, I asked Mr. Barker if he would take a chair and have some with us; and so polite he was, jumping up to fetch the kettle for me to fill the teapot, and handing the bread and butter directly I finished, talking very pleasant all the time. And there sat William as quiet as a mouse, eating his tea as if he hadn't a word to say —he that can have his say well enough when he pleases. Mr. Barker asked him questions, and he

only kind o' growled out an answer, and I sits
wondering what on earth ailed him, I never see him
so glum. Mr. Barker went off after tea, and Will
sits himself down by the fire and pretended to read.
He wouldn't talk to me or the children, so I let
him alone, thinking I'd have it out with him by
and bye. So when he'd got comfortable in bed,
and I was doing some little matters about the
room, I says, 'Why, whatever made you so glum
to-night, old man?'"

"'Just as if you didn't know,' says he.

"'Me!' says I, 'what do you mean?'

"'Oh yes, indeed,' says he, 'just as if you didn't;
I daresay it's very fine to sit there at table and be
waited on like a duchess. And its "Oh, Mrs.
Matthews, let me get the kettle," and "Mrs. Matthews, shall I cut some bread and butter?" Very
fine indeed, but I don't like it, mind you, so there.'

"'Why, old fellow, you don't mean as you are
jealous?' And for the life of me, ma'am, I couldn't
help laughing; to think of Will being jealous of a
dowdy old wife like me. Well, he said, he didn't
know about being jealous, but he didn't want to
see any man waiting on me. So I says, 'Well, if
you don't like no one to wait on me, you do it
yourself, old man; you get up and get me the
kettle yourself, and you'll see if I am likely to care

for anyone else doing it; and now go to sleep, and don't be such a donkey again.' You see, ma'am, if I've anything to say to Will, I bides my time and wait till he's safe in bed, and then I've my say out, and he can't run away."

"A very good way too," said Mrs. Wilson. "And is he quite got over his jealous fit?"

"Law, yes, ma'am, it wasn't likely to last, and I don't think it's a complaint he's subject to. But please, ma'am, I must get the children home again, and wish you and Miss Ellen good-day."

The children were called from their play, and were only partially consoled for being fetched away by the present of a pot of jam for their supper, and the promise that little Miss Nelly should come and see them the next time her aunt went into their neighbourhood.

Mrs. Matthews and the children reached home rather late, and found father and the boys on the look-out for them. Father took up Polly in his arms, and had to listen to a long account of the grand game of play she and Nelly had been having, and the big doll that had real shoes and real stockings.

"And there was another Nelly, father, who had such pretty cheeks, and her hair curled, oh, so long! Why don't my hair curl?" And clapping her

hands, " there's something so good in there," pointing to the pot, "and Georgy and Jim's to have
some."

" Bless the child! how fast your tongue goes ;
ain't I to have something good too ? " asked her
father.

Oh yes! father was to have some, and Polly was
going to sit on his knee and have some supper.

The boys were quite ready for their share of the
feast, and while they discussed the contents of the
pot, which was a very unusual accompaniment to
their supper, Jane told her husband of her visit,
and how she had seen little Miss Nelly Lee.

" Missus doesn't get out so much now as she was
used to ; she and Miss Ellen was as kind as ever,
and asked after you, Will, and was so glad to hear
the boys were doing well."

" Ah, they are very kind," said William ; "but
now, children, mother's tired, so, Nelly, put Polly
to bed ; and, boys, be off."

" I don't half like the feel of my leg," said Jane ;
" the walk's tired it, I suppose."

Jane had been troubled with a bad leg a great
part of her life, and often was obliged to rest it
when she would gladly have been engaged with
more active work. Her constitution was not origi-
nally strong, and the rough treatment and scanty

food she had in her childhood had not made it
stronger. Her weakness showed itself, as it so
often does, in the leg; and some year or two after
the last recorded visit to Mrs. Wilson, it became so
very bad, and she was altogether so much out of
health that the doctor strongly advised her to go
into the hospital, where she would have perfect
rest.

"I know you," said Mr. Miles, "what a bustling
body you are; and unless you are almost tied up
you won't be quiet. Here is this good little lassie
of yours, I know she will do her best to keep house
while you are laid by, won't you?"

Nelly thought she could, she was sure she would
try; and mother did let her do most of the cleaning
now her leg was bad.

Mr. Miles had a great respect for Jane, whom he
had known for many years, so he left her, promising
he would speak to the house surgeon of St. Bar-
tholomew's, and get a recommendation for her as
an in-patient.

Poor Jenny! it was a great trial to leave her
home, but when she found how the idea upset her
husband, she pretended that it was just what she
wanted, and made quite light of it.

"Poor old fellow!" she said to her neighbour,
Mrs. Barker, "we ain't never been parted, and he's

that cut up, I can't bear to go ; but then, if I don't, maybe I shall lose my leg altogether, and that 'ud be worse still." She had the comfort of knowing all would go on as well as could be expected at home, during her absence, for she had brought up the children to be very helpful. The boys had been accustomed to be up betimes, to light the fire, set the kettle on, and clean their boots before they set off for their work in the morning.

Jane used to say, " She could have done it all herself a deal easier, but the work did them more good than harm, and spared her strength."

The boys were so fond of her, that they did not seem ever to think anything done for mother was a hardship. Mrs. Barker promised to look in and help Nelly in such matters as were beyond her powers, and Nelly was to see after Polly, who was rather a wilful little woman ; and if her mother had let her, would rule everybody in the house. After having provided for everything as far as possible, Jane got her husband to take her to the hospital.

" Good-bye, dear old Will," said she, " please God I shall come back again strong enough to whip you all round ; and don't be down-hearted. What a thing it is there should be such a beautiful place to go to : and you are to come and see me ; and do go and tell Miss Wilson where I am, I'm sure she'll come and see me."

William promised he would, and giving her a hearty kiss, left her, feeling very disconsolate and lonely.

"Please, ma'am," said Mrs. Wilson's servant to her, "there's a man at the door wants to see you or Miss Wilson; he's says his name is Matthews."

"Tell him to walk up," said Mrs. Wilson. "I hope," said she, turning to her daughter, "there's nothing wrong with Jane or the children, she did not look at all well when she was last here."

"Well, William, how are you? It's many a day since I saw you. And how is the wife and the children?"

"Why, ma'am," said William, "my missus is laid up and gone to the hospital; she bid me come and ask miss if so be she'd go and see her. I'd take it very kind of you, miss."

Of course, Miss Wilson agreed to go as soon as she could. Both she and her mother were very sorry to hear the cause, and did their best to comfort William.

"Thank'ee, ma'am," said William, "I know it's for her good; but the place do look so cold like without her, there ain't many like Jane; we never had an ill word since we was married."

"What a blessing that is to think of," said Mrs. Wilson; "but we must not forget, my friend, who sends these trials—'Whom He loveth He chasteneth.' It is hard for you now, I know; but try and think of the goodness of God in giving you a good wife, and trust Him to restore her to you and the children. Depend upon it, there is a blessing even in this trial; but it is to those that love Him that all things work together for good. You must not let your faith fail now, when you want it most, and try and keep up your spirits for the children's sake."

"Thank'ee, ma'am," said William, "you are very good; and I'll try and not be down-hearted. The young 'uns follow their mother, and does all they can, poor things. Good evening, ma'am—good evening, miss, and thank'ee kindly. Jane will be main glad to see you."

The next day, Miss Wilson started on her visit to the hospital; but as Jane's home was only a little out of the direct way, she called there in order that she might give Jane the latest news from home. It was a fine, brisk, frosty day, and Miss Wilson enjoyed her walk. She found Nelly very busy, washing up the dinner things in quite a womanly style, the room quite tidy, and Polly sitting on a stool doing something with a needle

F

and thread. Miss Wilson was asked to guess what
it was; but that being an effort which, from its
appearance, was beyond her power, she was told in
a whisper, as a great secret, that it was a kettle-
holder for mother when she came home. She told
them she was going to see mother, and should tell
her what good girls she had, and how busy they
were—promising faithfully not to say a word of
the kettle-holder. She was leaving the house, when
a neighbour came running in to see if William was
in; he was to tell him that George had broken his
leg by a fall from a ladder, and he had been carried
to the hospital. Miss Wilson was obliged to stay
a little longer to console the children, and then left,
wondering whether Jane had heard of the accident,
and resolving to make enquiries before she saw her.
Close by the gates she met William, who looked in
a maze, as he had only just heard something was
amiss, and did not know what.

"Oh, miss, I'm so glad to meet you," said he,
"I'm just going to see the poor boy, if they'll let
me in."

"Well," said Miss Wilson, "we can but ask."

They found their way in, and in answer to the
question—Was a boy, named Matthews, badly
hurt; and could they see him?—were answered,
that the boy was then under the surgeon's hands;

he had a compound fracture of the leg, and if they liked to wait till he was in bed, as the man was his father, he could see him—and the lady would be admitted also. William was very eager she should see him, as he begged her to tell his wife, "he couldn't."

A gentleman now came through the room where they were waiting, who remarked to another who followed, "Capital little chap, that; bore it like a brick—he'll do well."

"Please, sir," said William, "was that my boy—Matthews, sir?"

"Faith! I don't know! But stay, I think that was his name; a bricklayer's boy, fell off a ladder, and fortunately broke his leg when he might have broken his neck."

"Oh yes, sir, that's him."

"Ah, well, my man, don't fret, he'll do; brave boy, didn't cry out once."

"Thank you kindly, sir," said William; and much relieved that it was no worse, he and Miss Wilson followed the attendant to the ward in which he was placed.

George looked pale, but a smile overspread his face at the sight of his father.

"I'm so glad you are come," said he; "what will mother say? Oh, Miss Wilson, do please tell her

I ain't bad, you know ; and the doctor says I shall
soon be all right if I lie still. Poor mother, she'll
be so sorry."

Poor Georgie! all his thoughts seemed to be for
his mother ; and he was comforted when Miss
Wilson assured him she would carry her a good
account of him.

"But how did it happen, my boy?"

"I don't rightly know," said he ; "but the man
as I works under—Jackson, you know, father!"
His father nodded. "Well, he's a kind of hasty
feller ; and he sung out from the scaffold for a hod
of bricks. It wasn't quite my work, miss, but he
seemed in a hurry like, so I ketched up the hod as
fast as I could, and got half-way up the ladder ;
when, somehow, I slipped like, and down the bricks
fell, and me a-top of 'em."

"They shouldn't 'a let him done it," muttered
Will, "but he always was such a willin' little chap."

"Well, George," said Miss Wilson, "it is indeed
a mercy it was no worse ; and I hope before you
go to sleep you will pray to God and thank Him
for having saved your life. You had better not
talk any more now, but I shall come in a day or
two and see you again ; now I am going to see
your mother."

"Good-bye, ma'am ; and good-bye, father. When

you come again, bring me my own little Testament,
and give my love to Nelly and Polly."

Matthews left the ward and turned to go home,
while Miss Wilson went into the women's side, and
was directed to the ward in which Jane was.

" Oh, miss," said she, " I knowed you'd come, and
I am so glad to see you."

" Oh, it is very fine of you, Jane, to be laid up
here like a lady, taking your ease indeed," said
Miss Wilson cheerfully. " I was so sorry to hear
from William of your being here, because I knew
you must be bad before you would give up."

" Why, yes, miss, I did it for the best ; and the
doctors here say I might have lost my leg altogether if I hadn't ; it wouldn't have been right,
miss, to be made a cripple, if it could anyways be
helped. It's leaving the father and the children as
fidgets me most."

" Ah ! but you must not be too anxious about
them," said Miss Wilson. And then she told her
how she had been to see them, and how well Nelly
was doing, and Polly was behaving like a lady.
Jane was naturally much interested in all the little
details Miss Wilson gave her. They seemed to
cheer her, but her friend could not help observing
that with all her efforts to look bright, she was weak,
and she rather dreaded the effect that the knowledge

of George's accident might have upon her. Still, it
was useless to delay, her time was getting short,
and she would be obliged to go home; so in the
kindest and most considerate way she told Jane
all about it. Poor thing, she was very much cut
up; and "Poor Georgie! my poor boy!" was all
she could say through her tears. She could not
help it, and she had a good cry.

There was a general feeling of sympathy from
the women occupying the beds near hers. Miss
Wilson did her best to console her; and the first
burst of grief over, Jane's healthy nature helped her
to turn to the brightest side.

"What a comfort it was you was there, miss!
and I know you've told me the worst."

"Yes, indeed, Jane," said Miss Wilson, "it would
not be kind to hide anything from you; your trust
in me would be gone. I don't like to magnify
evils or make things out worse than they are; but
I do love truth, and you know me too well to
dream of my deceiving you."

"Yes, indeed, miss; and you'll come again
soon?"

"Well, I'll try and come as soon as I can, but
now I must go." So stooping down, Miss Wilson
kissed her, whispering, "'No chastening for the
present seemeth to be joyous; nevertheless, after-

ward it yieldeth the peaceable fruit of righteousness
to them that are exercised thereby.' Let us trust
our Good Shepherd, Jenny."

A hearty squeeze of the hand was her answer,
and Miss Wilson went away, and at the gate she
found William, waiting to hear how "the old
woman" was.

"She was a good deal upset about George, but
she bears up bonnily, and is looking forward in
good hopes of getting back home all the better for
being where she is," said Miss Wilson. "And now
you had better go home and tell the little ones how
glad their mother was to hear of their being such
good children."

"God bless you, miss; I'll go now, and thank
you."

It was a fortunate circumstance for our friend
Jenny, that she had the free use of her hands, and
when comfortably propped up in bed she could
work at her ease. She had foreseen that she should
be able to do so, and had, therefore, provided herself with work to take into the hospital with her,
such as a new shirt for her husband, and one for
each of the boys. The materials for new garments
stopped there, for money was not plentiful; but
there were many cuttings and contrivings known
to thrifty mothers, that had to be done for the girls,
which kept her hands well employed.

The bed next to hers, on one side, was occupied
by a young woman named Charlotte Tyler, who
was suffering from a bad swelling on the knee.
She was getting better when Mrs. Matthews came
into the hospital; but though she could sit up in
bed, she seemed to have no idea she could do anything with her hands; and as she was not able to
read, the time was so wearisome that it was no
wonder she became very fretful.

"Laws! how you do work away, Mrs. Matthews,"
said Charlotte one day, after watching her a long
time in silence; "one would say you was a-working
for a wager. I think there's a lot of work to do
when one's well, and there ain't no call to do it in
the 'ospital, where one comes to be quiet."

"Well," replied Jane, "the quiet is very nice, but
one may have too much of a good thing, and I
should fret if I could not do anything. I am so
thankful I can use my hands, my bit of work makes
the time pass more quickly. It's funny you and I
should be so close together, both with lame legs.
What made yours bad?"

"It was kneeling on those horrid cold stones,
that has to be kept so prim and white," said
Charlotte. "I lived housemaid in one of them big
houses by the Bank, that has stone stairs from top
to bottom of the house, and long stone passages.

They took a heap of time to clean, but precious little to get dirty; and missus was particular and couldn't a-bear to see a speck of dirt, so I was kep' at it from morning to night scrubbing, and lots of work besides. I was used to go to bed that tired I couldn't sleep; and when my knee got bad, I was ready to cry with the pain, and cook told the missus how bad it was, and she told the master, who was a doctor; so he looked at it, and directly he saw it he said he knowed I had been kneeling too much on cold stones, and asked me if I had used to kneel upon anything soft, and I couldn't help saying ' No, I had a bit o' carpet on purpose, but when I was in a hurry I forgot it, and I didn't think it 'ud hurt me.' Master was a peppery gentleman, and said I shouldn't be such a fool as to fancy things wouldn't hurt me, as was bad for other people; and I'd got myself in a nice scrape, for I must go to the hospital, and it was great odds if I was ever fit to scrub again."

"Well, never mind that," said Mrs. Matthews, "if you can't scrub again, you can do something else, I'll be bound."

"I don't know, I'm sure," replied Charlotte. " You see, I ain't got any friends in Lunnon to go to when I get out of the hospital; and my wages will soon go if I get a lodgin', and then I only knows housemaid's work, and master said I mustn't do hard work in a hurry again, and I don't think I could if I tried ever so much."

"Are you fond of children?" asked Jane. "Couldn't you try for a nursemaid's place?"

"Oh, I'm fond enough of children; but then a nursemaid is always expected to do needlework, and I'm no hand at that."

"There's no reason why you shouldn't be," said Jane; "see how white your hands are getting from resting so long. Now, when nurse comes round again we'll get her to set you up in bed as nicely as she does me, and then I'll do my best to set you in the way to do needlework. Why, bless you! I was a'most as old as you before I knew how myself, and I've earned many a shilling by my needle before now; at any rate, it will be of use some time, whatever you get to do."

The girl's face brightened up with a new hope, and it was evident that a change from doing nothing was a welcome idea, and she thanked Mrs. Matthews heartily for her promised help.

"But I ain't got anything to do here in the way of work, not a thimble even."

"Never mind," said her friend, "I brought my bag with me; and I can give you something to begin upon, and a thimble too; I always have a

spare one, it's so handy. Look here, these is bits
of patchwork; my Nelly's done all this, and very
well done it is for her age. Some day I shall have
quite a handsome quilt. Miss Wilson, that kind
lady who came to tell me about my poor boy,
promised to bring me some pretty pieces for it, and
I expect her every day. Perhaps you'll be able to
do some of it, for it's easy work and straight-
forward; and I'll fix it and teach you to fix for
yourself."

"Well, you are kind, to be sure; and here comes
nurse," said Charlotte. "Oh! please, nurse, do set
me up in bed; this good woman is going to give
me some work."

"Well, I'm glad to hear that," said the nurse;
"you will get well as fast again, and pick up your
spirits into the bargain. You can't do better than
follow Mrs. Matthews' advice; see what a busy bee
she is, and how neatly she works," continued the
nurse, taking the collar of a shirt Jane had just
finished stitching.

"There, now you are nicely fixed, I know; and
you won't be half so tired to-night as you were last
night, and not quite so out of sorts either," added
the nurse laughing.

Charlotte Tyler sat to work with a will; she was
sadly awkward at first, as she said, "Her fingers

were all thumbs." But she got on famously by degrees; and the occupation amused and interested her so much, that she lost her fretfulness, and quite acknowledged that doing nothing was not so pleasant in reality as she thought it would be before she tried it.

Miss Wilson, true to her word, soon came again to see Jane, and brought her news of her children. They were all well, and Miss Wilson made Jane laugh by her description of Nelly getting up the wash.

"There was the little thing ironing away so busily, she did not even hear me go in; and I stood and watched her till Miss Polly caught sight of me, and then of course there was no more quiet, and we were obliged to have a game of play. She had been ironing too, Nelly told me; but she had been careful not to let her have a hot iron. I stayed," continued Miss Wilson, "while Nelly laid the cloth for dinner, and William came in. He looks well, and was very glad to find I was coming to see you. There is a mysterious little packet I promised to give you; I have no idea what is in it, but Jim and the girls were busy doing it up in a corner, while I was talking to their father."

"Why, bless me!" exclaimed Jane, "what have the children been after? What a pretty useful pincushion, and what is written on it? 'For mother's bag, from Nelly.' Well, now, how neat it is made, I do think you must have helped her, miss."

"Perhaps I did, a little," said Miss Wilson smiling; "I fixed it, but it is all her own work. I did not know she had sent it though, I fancied it was to be given to you when you returned home, but I suppose it would not keep till then. This is an original packet—Polly's, I should guess."

Jane opened another little parcel, very queerly packed, and found it to contain a stick of barley sugar, a biscuit, and some bull's eyes.

"That must be Polly, surely," said her mother. "Bless the child, to send me what she's so fond of herself. Here's another, it feels like money."

Written outside the third enclosure was, "Jim's first wages for mother."

It was half-a-crown. Jane looked enquiringly at Miss Wilson, while tears stood in her eyes.

"Yes," replied her friend, "it is quite true; Jim proves so handy a boy and so steady, that the foreman spoke of him to the master, and Mr. Sandars was very kind, and told Jim himself that he always liked to encourage steady lads, and he was willing to keep him, and he should have half-a-crown a-week for the present."

"Oh, I am so glad, miss; and now he will keep

with his father and be out of harm's way. I wish
my poor George had been," continued Jane, "and
then perhaps he would not have broken his leg."

"Well, but he is getting on very well, I hear;
and at his age, bones soon mend. You see," said
Miss Wilson, "I brought you bad news the last
time I came, so I am doubly pleased to be the
bearer of good news to-day. And now I want to
know how you are yourself."

"Thank ye, miss, I am getting on pretty well,"
replied Jane. "I've a deal of medicine to take, and
the leg is not healed yet, but that could not be
expected, the doctor says. I feel better in myself,
though, and I think I'm getting on quite as well as
I could expect, considering I haven't been here
very long."

"And have you pleasant neighbours?" enquired
Miss Wilson; "here seems one able to employ
herself," continued she, turning to Charlotte Tyler;
"and I should think, my friend, you find it a comfort to be able to use your fingers. I suppose you
are getting better."

"Thank ye, ma'am, I'm a deal better; but I
never thought of doing anything till Mrs. Matthews
put it into my head; and the time ain't near so
long now as it used to be. Mrs. Matthews was so
busy like, you see, ma'am," continued Charlotte, "I

got ashamed to be doing nothing when I could work. But I'm a poor hand at it yet.'

"Indeed, ma'am," said Jane, "she is getting on very well, poor thing! and is going to help me with my quilt soon."

"Ah, and that reminds me, Jenny," said Miss Wilson, "that I have some pieces for you in my pocket. Here they are, but you must keep them to look at when I'm gone, for my time will be getting short. Who is your neighbour on the other side, with her head so covered in bandages?"

"Indeed, ma'am," replied Jane, "I don't rightly know. She was carried in two days ago; and I think, from what the nurse said, her husband had ill-used her. She moans dreadfully, at night especially; and I think she was quite off her head last night, for she cried out so, 'Oh, don't, Tom! don't!' so often."

"Poor woman!" said Miss Wilson, "how sad these things are!"

"Ah, they are indeed, miss," said Jane; "there are many sad sights and sounds in a hospital, but then again it's a grand thing to be able to have the first of advice and nursing free gratis for nothing: so we must put one thing against another and be thankful. Only, miss, it does seem so puzzling why God, who is so good, let such horrid things be.

One can understand an accident like my boy's, which was an accident, and nobody's fault like; and then an illness seems natural like, and what we must expect at times; but a man ill-using his wife, especially if she's a quiet body, as this poor soul looks, it fairly beats me; it don't seem like Him who gave His own dear Son for us, and must love us poor things so much."

"Ah, Jane, that is a subject that has troubled wiser heads than yours or mine," said Miss Wilson. "I only know it is quite impossible to understand our heavenly Father's dealings with His creatures: why, even your little Polly could not understand why you make her do many things you know it is right she should do; so it is not so wonderful if we do not comprehend God's ways. But we do know that 'God is love;' it is impossible to doubt that blessed fact, everything in nature around us proves it, even if we had not the word of God itself to teach us. Therefore, I think we may rest quite satisfied that He permits such sad things to be, for some wise purpose that is hid from our sight, because it would not be good for us to know. Yet even as it is, we can see some use in these sad things; when they lead us to pity such poor, misguided creatures so much, that we feel obliged to try and help them to become better, and so we learn to love our neighbour better; and as we learn to love our neighbour more, we are led to love God Himself more. St. John, you know, says a man is a liar, who says he loves God and yet hates his brother: for 'He that loveth not his brother whom he hath seen, how can he love God whom he hath not seen?' So, you see, we really dare not say we love God if we do not love our brother or neighbour; and if we love any one, we try and keep them out of harm's way, do we not?"

"Why, yes, miss, certainly we do," replied Jane; "but it is very hard to know how to do it."

"So it is, indeed," said Miss Wilson; "but the will is the thing that is mostly wanted, the way would soon come if the will was there—or perhaps I should say, if people thought on the matter. My dear mother has often said, that 'we take wickedness as we do fevers, as something that must be.' But doctors say, if people were temperate and cleanly, and let in plenty of light and air into their houses, fevers would vanish. Now, wickedness of all kinds is dirt and pollutes the soul, and must be got rid of by letting in the light of God's Holy Word, and by cultivating love, truth, and honesty, and cultivating good temper and kindness to each other; in fact, making goodness more attractive

G

than wickedness. Good will overcome evil in the
end, and then the kingdom of God will be come,
and His will be done, as we pray it may in the
Lord's prayer: and in the meantime, the wheat
and the tares must grow together."

"Well, I suppose they must, miss," replied Jane.
"It is God's will, and that ought to be enough for
poor creatures like us. I am a bit more satisfied
to think that if God lets evil be done here now, it
is for a wise reason."

"Ah, Jenny," said Miss Wilson, "depend upon
it, things very dark to our sight now, will be made
clear as daylight by and by. And there is great
comfort in the promise that 'all things work
together for good to them that love Him.' Now,
I really must say good-bye for to-day; mamma
will think I am lost, and she was not very well
when I left her."

"And to think," exclaimed Jane, "that I have
been so full of my own concerns, I never asked
after her; I can't think how I could forget. I
hope you won't take it amiss, miss; I should have
thought of her directly your back was turned."

"Ah, well, I forgive you this once, Jenny," said
Miss Wilson smiling; "forgetting an old friend is
a new complaint with you; and she is not ill, only
a little fagged, and wants rest. Perhaps if I talked

as much to her as I have to-day to you, I should have tired her out as I may have done you."

"Ah, no fear of that, miss," said Jane. "Please give my duty to missus, and I hope you will be able to come and see me again soon."

"I shall try, certainly," replied Miss Wilson; "and now, good-bye. I shall try and see the children on my way home, if I have time."

"Thank ye, miss; and could not Mrs. Barker bring them to see me? I do so long for them. And I want," continued Jane, "to ask Mrs. Barker if she could take this young woman in as a lodger for a week or two. She expects to be discharged soon, and has nowhere to go to."

"What, you mean your neighbour here?" enquired Miss Wilson.

"Yes, sure, miss; and perhaps you might hear of a light place for her. I do think she is a tidy girl," said Jane.

"I suppose you could have a character from your last place?" enquired Miss Wilson, turning to Charlotte.

"Oh yes, ma'am," said Charlotte; "I lived a year with Mrs. King, of Bank Buildings, and only left because I was ill; the work was very heavy."

"I can well believe that," replied Miss Wilson; "I know Mrs. King very well, and I am sure she will speak well of you if you deserved it. I will remember you, and see if I can find anything for you. And now, good-bye." And off she went, at a good pace, with the satisfactory feeling of having given pleasure to two people, at least.

"What a nice lady that is!" remarked Charlotte, "she talks so cheerful and looks so pleasant."

"Ah, she is indeed," replied Jane; "and she is as good as she looks. It's my opinion, if there was more Miss Wilsons in the world it would be a deal better place than it is. If ever she had to find fault with me, she did it without being cross. Some people, if they have to find fault, have a knack of making one angry with them, instead of yourself."

"Ah! don't they, just?" said Charlotte; "just like my master, he used to blow us up all round, and we couldn't a-bear him; and I'm sure it didn't make any of us a bit better."

"Ah, there's a deal of power in the 'soft word,'" said Jane, "as, thank God, I learned a long time ago."

Miss Wilson paid many more visits to the hospital during Mrs. Matthews' stay. She generally found her bed surrounded with those of the patients who could get about. It had become well known that Jane was an authority in the matter of cutting out and fashioning garments. She was always ready to lend an ear to any little trouble, and could contrive little things to amuse a wearied child, and there were several children in the ward, for this was before the days of children's hospitals. It was no wonder that when she was pronounced fit to go home, there was a general feeling of regret from her fellow-patients. She was in the hospital fully six weeks, and, thanks to the excellent treatment she had had, she looked quite a different being, and merited her husband's remark, that, "except being perhaps a trifle washy-looking, she looked as if she had been ground young again." Her boy George got home only a short time before her, for the bones of his leg had not united so soon as the surgeon expected. He was rather a delicate boy, and in constitution as well as appearance took a good deal after his mother. Notwithstanding good nursing and skilful treatment, under one of the cleverest surgeons, the leg became somewhat shortened, causing him to limp in his walk.

There had been great preparations made at home for Jane's return. Her husband, aided by Jim, had been busy working after-hours, whitewashing the ceilings and papering the keeping-room. He knew Jane had long wanted such little matters done, so he determined to give her an agreeable surprise.

Their kind neighbour, Mrs. Barker, had looked in
from time to time to see after the cleaning up.
Charlotte Tyler was lodging with her for a few
days before she went to the place Miss Wilson had
fortunately found for her. She was a great assistance to Nelly in the heavier part of the cleaning,
and worked away with a will, happy in any way to
show her sense of the kindness Jenny had shown
her in the hospital.

Good little Nelly was very anxious everything
should be in apple-pie order. Polly, not to be out-
done, was found diligently washing the back yard,
mounted on her mother's pattens, and handling a
broom considerably taller than herself, having pre-
viously deluged the place with water she had
contrived to upset from a pail unfortunately placed
in her way. Of course she was in a state of dirt,
that caused poor Nelly almost to despair of making
her fit to be seen again. Happily, she came to no
further harm than a thorough washing could set to
rights ; and being very penitent, she promised her
father, when he and Jim started to fetch mother
home, that she would sit on her own little stool,
" like a lady," till he came back.

"And you try and keep your word," said her
father ; "for what would mother say, if she found
we had changed our Polly into a dirty little sweep
while she was away?"

Such a direful idea made so strong an impression, that she really kept her word pretty well, taking great credit to herself for it afterwards, being several times overheard to boast herself of "having kept it like a lady," meaning her promise.

Happy is the family in which the mother's return home is as eagerly expected as it was in Jane's modest home. Very thankful was she to find herself once more seated by her own fireside, with her children round her, and her husband looking at her with great content. He declared "home looked like itself again now his old woman was in her place once more."

There was no lack of conversation, there was so much to ask and so much to tell, and the new paper to be admired ; but the greatest delight of all, to Jane's motherly heart, was to see her boy George again, and to hear from his own lips all the details of his accident. She thought him looking but weakly, though he declared he was quite himself again and all ready for work, "only father would not let me try for any till you was come home."

" Ah," said his father, "he wanted to be off, but the doctor bid me be careful of him ; so we thought we'd wait till the mother comed home, though he did think it a bit hard that he couldn't earn anything, like master Jim here."

"Never mind," said his mother, "all in good time ; we must look out for something lighter than bricklaying for him. I was pleased to have your half-crown," Jim," continued she, "and I don't mean to spend it either. It did me a deal of good to hear you was with father, and was a good boy."

"I means to try my best," answered Jim. "Why, you know, mother, it warn't every master 't would speak to a youngster like me ; but Mr. Sandars was very kind, and told me he hoped I should be as steady, and be a good workman like father ; so I told him," continued Jim, speaking bravely, "I wasn't going to disgrace my name if I know'd it. He's a brick, he is ; and I only hope poor Georgy will get a master like him."

"I am sure I hope so too," replied his mother. "But now, Nelly, I've been so took up with the boys, I've hardly had a look at you, and my Polly too. How busy you must have been to make the place look so nice !"

"Yes, indeed," said her father ; "Nelly makes a capital little housekeeper."

"Well, father," said Nelly, "you know mother taught me, and I tried to do my best ; but I'm so glad you've come back again. I got so afraid sometimes that things would go wrong, but father was very good and didn't scold, though I did spoil the dinner once, and clean forgot to boil the potatoes another time."

".Accidents will happen sometimes with wiser folks than my Nelly," said her mother; " and I am glad you managed so well."

Polly had been seated on her mother's lap, wonderfully quiet for her; but there being a slight lull in the stream of conversation, she considered her turn was fully come. She had been carefully cuddling up something in her hand, but now she seized her opportunity, and triumphantly produced the kettle-holder. If it was not perfection in her mother's estimation it decidedly was in her own. It really was a very respectable-made affair for such a little thing to do, and her mother praised it, and gave the required promise, that she should use that always at tea-time, and George undertook to drive in a nail by the fire-place on which it was to be hung.

There was quite a little feast for supper in honour of mother's return; and, under Mrs. Barker's superintendence, Nelly had made a beef-steak pudding, which was pronounced a most successful performance, and gave great satisfaction; so much so, that it was all finished; and Nelly was quite delighted when her mother said she thought "in time she might be a good cook."

"And now, father," said Jane, "let's have a chapter before we goes to bed."

"Oh, yes," cried Polly, who was very wide awake; "and me and Nelly is going to sing such a pretty hymn, Miss Wilson teached me; she said we was to sing it when you comed home."

"That was very good of her," said her mother; "but now father's going to read, so come, Polly, and sit in my lap."

William read the fourteenth chapter of St. John, and all afterwards kneeling down, they thanked God for His mercy in bringing them together again in health. It was a very simple but earnest prayer, and concluded with a petition that what they asked might be granted to them for Jesus' sake. The girls then sang their hymn, to a tune Mrs. Wilson had composed for that suitable for children :—

> " Lord, I have passed another day,
> 　　And come to thank Thee for Thy care,
> Forgive my faults in work or play,
> 　　And listen to my evening prayer."

It sounded very pretty from their sweet young voices, and was followed by the evening hymn, in which they all joined, so concluding a very happy evening.

The next morning the family were early astir, and Matthews and Jim went to their work, leaving

strong injunctions that mother was not to be
allowed to do too much. Jane laughed and said,
"She wasn't cut out for a lady quite, but she'd try
and see how lazy she could be." So when household matters were set pretty straight, she and
George sat down comfortably to consult over his
getting something to do.

"You see, mother, I can limp about pretty tidy,
though I'm pretty glad to rest my leg when I've
been standing a bit."

"I should think that's likely enough," said his
mother; "why, you can't expect to get a broken
leg quite strong in six weeks."

"You don't think I need go back to Thompson's
yard, mother, do you? I daresay master might
take me on again, but I get all of a tremble thinking of going up a ladder. I don't want to be a
sneak, mother," continued the poor boy, "and I'll
try it again if you think I ought to."

"No, I don't want you to, my chap," replied his
mother; "I never rightly liked it for you. I think
we had better enquire about here for some light
work. Laws! something is sure to turn up at the
right time. Maybe Mr. Miles will be going by in
a day or so; he promised to give me a call when I
came out of the hospital, and he's a gentleman as
keeps his word; and then who knows, he may

think of something as may be fit for you, he knows such lots of people. You needn't be idle now neither, you can do some writin' and summing. A lad ain't worth much as can't do that."

"You're about right there, mother," replied George ; "and if I can get Polly to sit quiet a bit, perhaps I can get her to learn her letters ; do ye hear, young 'un? Come, and we'll play at school, and you shall learn all about great A, little A, bouncing B."

Brother George was a great favourite with the little woman, as he was always ready to contrive toys for her and carry her pick-a-back. The notion of learning her letters seemed a brilliant idea ; and she set to work with such a will, that she learnt pretty well half the alphabet before dinner, and of course was eager to exhibit her learning to her father, who was very ready to praise the industry of his little maid.

Mrs. Matthews paid a visit to her neighbour, Mrs. Barker, to thank her for looking after the children. She found Charlotte Tyler packing her box ready to send off by the carrier to her new place at Hampstead. Miss Wilson had taken some pains to find a place for her that would not be too trying. Mrs. King had given her a good character, as an honest, hard-working girl, only she was careless. Mrs. King had blamed herself for not looking to see that she used the kneeling-mat she had provided for the housemaid's use; but really it did seem too bad, that girls were so thoughtless and required looking after like babies.

"I am afraid," said she, "that the poor girl has had a sharp lesson, and I hope she will profit by it. My husband says she has been suffering from what is known as the 'housemaid's knee;' and it is generally brought on by kneeling on cold stones, without taking proper care to protect the knee sufficiently, by using a mat or carpet to kneel on."

Charlotte was really grateful to Miss Wilson for the trouble she had taken about her, and promised faithfully she would do her best and try to be more careful in future. She told Jane she didn't know but getting into the hospital had been the best thing that could have happened to her; for she'd learnt a many things she never know'd afore, "besides meeting with a dear good soul like you, Mrs. Matthews. And here's Mrs. Barker, she's so good to me; why, she won't let me pay for my bed! only just for my board! She says it ain't nice for a girl to go to a place without a penny in her pocket; and my clothes used to cost such a deal, I never could save anything."

"Ah," said her friend, "now you can work so

much better, you will be able to make your own clothes, besides mending up your old ones; and then you must try and lay by for a rainy day."

"Well, I'll see," replied Charlotte; "there's one thing, I'm not to have near the hard work I've been used to, and that's a save to one's clothes. Mrs. Burlton seems a nice lady, and the house looks like print, and she was very particular I should look neat, she said. I'm to have a holiday every three months, and then I shall come and see you, and tell you how I get on."

"Well, good-bye now," said Jane; "I fancy it must be tea-time. Good-bye, Mrs. Barker; it was good of you to take Charlotte in."

"Good evening, Mrs. Matthews, I'm glad to see you looking better; and as to Charlotte here," said Mrs. Barker, "I'm sure she's very welcome, and you'd have done the same twenty times over, so don't go to say nothing more about that."

Some days went on, and nothing offered suitable for George. Jane was getting anxious, and the poor boy rather down-hearted. Money was scarce, as the whole family had to depend on William's wages and the trifle Jim earned. They had been without lodgers for some little time, and of course money did not go quite so far while Jane was from home as she made it do when she was able to

manage herself. The children wanted shoes, and
many other little matters that mothers so well know
are needed in a family ; moreover, she was anxious
Nelly should have some more schooling. When
Mrs. Matthews made up her mind that such or
such a thing ought to be done, she rarely lost much
time in trying to do it. So, in the first place, she
told her husband he must look out for some
lodgers, for she was quite able to do for them now ;
and then, as she had not had a call from Mr. Miles,
she thought she would go and see him. She
remembered too that Miss Wilson had told her
she was welcome to a clothing ticket for the
clothing club to which Mrs. Wilson was secretary.
There were half-yearly sales of ready-made clothing
at cost price, which was a great advantage, and
Jane hoped to get some things that were much
wanted at the sale, which was near at hand. As
she could hardly walk so far herself, she got William
to take the girls with him and call on Mrs. Wilson
for the ticket. Nelly and Polly were always delighted to have a walk with father, and they were
very anxious to know if they should see little Miss
Nelly again.

Mrs. Wilson gladly gave William the ticket for
Jane, and recommended her to be early at the
room on the day of the sale, as she would then

have the best chance of getting what she required.
The children were very disappointed to find Miss
Nelly had gone home ; her mamma had been to
London and taken her back with her ; but they
brought home a few rather dilapidated toys she
had left behind, and George promised to mend
them up as good as new.

"The missus doesn't look any great shakes," said
William ; "and I doubt she ain't well. She asked
kindly after you and the boy, and bid me say she
should expect you to go and see her as soon as you
could manage so far. Miss wasn't at home, gone
for a change into the country, her ma' said."

"I'm glad of it," said his wife, "only the missus
is never quite happy when she's away. Now, I
say, George, you clean yourself up tidy, and you
and I'll go and see Mr. Miles ; and if he can't tell
us of anything, why," said Jane, "we'll get father
to ask Mr. Sandars to take you in at the foundry.
He don't like to because he's been so kind to Jim,
and it looks as if we was imposing on him."

"Well, one wouldn't like to do that," replied
George ; "and Jim 'ud crow over me just a bit at
first, as I'm oldest."

"I don't see that 't would matter much, and
besides you ain't there yet, at any rate," said his
mother ; "only it's well to have two strings to

one's bow, and if one thing won't do we must try another, and not sit still and suck our thumbs."

"You ain't one to do that, mother, not you," said George laughing.

Mr. Miles was not a chemist, though he had a shop. He was an elderly gentleman, of rather quaint appearance, and practised medicine as an apothecary; that is, he gave advice both at home and abroad, and kept a shop where he dispensed his medicines and sold drugs to chance customers. Apothecaries are an extinct race now; but in his day, Mr. Miles had an extensive practice, especially amongst his poorer neighbours, and was a really skilful man and very kind-hearted.

"Well, Mrs. Matthews, so you are in the land of the living. I was going to look in upon you, but, bless me! what with children down with the measles, and mothers upstairs with babies, I have had a hard time of it lately. And now," continued Mr. Miles, "how are you getting on? You didn't come home and find your children burnt to death, or your husband run away? You are a lucky woman then! But what is this lad doing here? he does not look over-bright."

Jane thanked the doctor for his enquiries, and then told him how she had been so bold as to come and ask his advice about George; for she did not think he was quite fit to go back to his old trade. Mr. Miles agreed with her on that point, and told her that he never ought to have been put to it.

"You see, my good woman," said he, "breaking his leg was a shock to his constitution, as we doctors call it ; and if he was a fine young gentleman we should send him to the sea-side, and make him take it easy for a bit, but of course you can't afford to do that."

"No, indeed, sir," replied Jane, "that would be impossible."

"Ah, well, you are not the only one that can't get everything that seems to be good for you," said Mr. Miles ; "and it's all for the best in the long run, depend upon it, though it is hard to see it at the time. Now, I will tell you what I can do for you. I want a boy I can depend upon, to carry out my medicine, clean boots and knives, and make himself generally useful in the house, and stay in the shop when he is not wanted elsewhere. It so happens I had to turn my boy away yesterday, as I found the young rascal playing pitch-and-toss in the street, instead of delivering some medicine that I was particularly anxious should reach a patient as quickly as possible. Loitering on an errand is an offence I never look over. So do you hear, my

lad ? If you come here, you are to come when you
are called, and do as you are bid."

George looked at his mother, and then at Mr.
Miles, with an expression on his face that clearly
meant that never should there be occasion of complaint on the score of his loitering over any work
or errand.

" What does your mother say ? " said Mr. Miles,
replying to George's look. " I see you would not
say no. The work is really light, none of my
patients live at a distance ; and there is no one in
the house but myself and my old housekeeper, and
if the boy gets on her blind side she would be
rather apt to pet and spoil him. He would have
two shillings a-week and plenty of grub, and just
now," continued Mr. Miles, in an undertone to
Jane, " that is very important for him, and maybe
the means of making him grow into a strong and
healthy man."

" Indeed, sir," said Jane, " I don't know how to
thank you enough for your kindness ; and I'm sure
his father and me will be thankful to let him come,
and many thanks to you. It don't do to boast of
one's own flesh and blood, but I am sure you may
trust George to do as he is told, for he's a good boy
at home, and I never know'd him to tell a lie in
his life."

"Well, let him come then at once," said Mr. Miles; "I know you, and I have known the boy off and on since he was a baby, so I needn't waste your time or mine by asking for character. You must keep him as tidy as you can, because the 'doctor's boy' is rather a cut above common errand boys, and should behave as such."

"Well, you see, sir," said Jane, "he's a growing lad, and it's hard to keep him in clean and decent clothes, but I'll do my best to make him nice."

"Very well, and I shall expect you here to-morrow morning by seven o'clock; and in the meantime I will talk to Mrs. Hudson, the housekeeper, and she will show you what to do before breakfast."

George said, "Thank ye, kindly, sir; and I'll be sure to be here in time." And then he and his mother returned home.

Jane was rather tired, though the distance was very short. She had some misgivings that her husband would not quite approve of George's engagement, but did not say so to the boy himself; for as she said to herself, "Time enough to damp his spirits when it can't be helped; and, maybe, after all, his father may like the place well enough."

True enough, William did object, because he didn't like boys dawdling about as errand boys, as it was a lazy kind of work, and it was better to bring up a boy to a trade.

"Yes," replied his wife, "that's true enough, Will; but I think it won't do him harm for a bit, and he may get a good friend in Mr. Miles."

"And you know, father," said George, who had been a little cast down by his father's objection, " I won't be a lazy boy: and only think! suppose I should break a leg again, shan't I be at the right shop to get it mended?"

Poor George! many a true word is spoken in jest. He had not been many months with Mr. Miles, before he had a fall in the street over a piece of orange peel, and did break his other leg. As the accident happened close to Mr. Miles' door, he was taken in there and his master set it for him, and then sent for his mother.

"Here's a pretty kettle of fish, Mrs. Matthews," said Mr. Miles. "I didn't bargain for that boy getting into mischief again."

"Oh! please, sir! what is the matter?" said Jane.

"Matter! why matter enough; he's been and broken his other leg: and it's my belief his bones are so brittle that he will be always at it. But there, don't take on about it," continued the kind-hearted Mr. Miles, seeing Jane turned very white;

"he is all right now, and my old woman has got him all comfortable in bed, and now she will be happy: only give Mrs. Hudson some one to nurse, and she is in her glory. So now you go upstairs and look after him yourself."

Jane was beginning to express her gratitude to Mr. Miles, but he cut her short by opening the door and pointing the way to the room George was in. There she found him comfortably in bed, eagerly looking for her.

"Oh, mother! you will say I'm an unlucky chap: but then, you see, this will just make my legs even, so don't you be cast down—and the master was so gentle with me," continued George, "and Mrs. Hudson too, she's like a mother."

"My poor boy," said Jane, kissing him; "if you are unlucky one way, you are lucky in getting good friends; I'm sure I don't know how to thank the master or Mrs. Hudson enough."

"Never you mind about that, Mrs. Matthews," said Mrs. Hudson, who just entered; "the boy's a good boy, and I'll look after him, so don't fret, but make your mind easy. I can't let you stay now, for he must try and go to sleep."

George was obliged to say good-bye to his mother, sending by her many messages to all at home. Jane left the room with Mrs. Hudson, who told her that the boy had behaved so well—had been so industrious and obliging, that she did not think Mr. Miles would ever make up his mind to part with him.

Time proved that Mrs. Hudson's opinion was correct. When George got about again, Mr. Miles proposed to his parents that he should stay with him altogether.

"He has plenty of brains," said he, "and has picked up a good deal of knowledge in the shop; and if he gives his mind to it, there is no reason why he may not in time become a druggist's assistant."

Matthews could not say anything against a plan that promised so well for the future welfare of his boy; and thankfully acknowledged Jane had not made a bad morning's work when she went to consult Mr. Miles about getting a place for him.

"Yes," said Jane, "it just proves that missus was right when she used to say, 'When you are in doubt, do the best you can, and put your trust in God.' And I'm sure we ought to be grateful to Him for His goodness to us and our children."

And here we may take leave of Jenny Matthews and her family, with a well-founded hope that God who had led her safely so far on life's journey, would be with her to the end. The Matthews family had neither wealth, rank, nor beauty, but they had what was of more worth, for they had a practical trust in God their Father; and they loved their neighbour, and, as far as was possible, lived in peace with all men.

It may be interesting to know that Jane is not a fictitious character, such as she was she is depicted in these pages. These memorials of her have been written to encourage those who are still fighting the battle of life. True, there are no wonderful events recorded of her daily life, no astounding adventures, but it is often the dull daily round of duties that is so irksome and so full of temptations to idleness, selfishness, and forgetfulness of God's commandments. Of such earnest, right-minded women as Jane Matthews (no matter in what station of life their lot may be placed), it may truly be said, "Her children arise up and call her blessed; her husband also, and he praiseth her."

Jarrold and Sons, Printers, Norwich.

PUBLISHED AT 7s. 6d.

George Gould, Rev. Sermons and Addresses by the late.
Together with a Memoir by his Son, GEORGE P. GOULD, M.A. With Photographic Portrait and View of the Interior of St. Mary's Chapel, Norwich.

Rambles of a Naturalist in Egypt and other Countries.
By J. H. GURNEY, JUN.

Six Thousand Illustrations of Moral and Religious Truths.
Tenth Edition, Revised and Enlarged. By JOHN BATE. Consisting of Definitions, Metaphors, Similes, Emblems, Contrasts, Analogies, Statistics, Synonyms, Anecdotes, &c., &c. Alphabetically arranged, with copious indices.

> "It is more useful to a preacher than an Encyclopædia, and far less costly."
> —*Literary World.*
> "It is without a compeer."—*Congregationalist.*
> "Many new Encyclopædias have succeeded it, but none have cut it out."
> —*Sword and Trowel.*

PUBLISHED AT 6s.

Alfreda Holme: A Story of Social Life in Australia.
By E. BOYD BAYLY. 8vo., 531 pages, cloth, elegant.

> "It is both graceful and pathetic, and is written with exquisite taste and expression."—*Daily Chronicle.*
> "A very pretty, bright, interesting book."—*Daily News.*
> "As a picture of Australian society, it has the merit of being obviously founded upon original observation."—*The Graphic.*

Observations on the Fauna of Norfolk.
By the late REV. RICHARD LUBBOCK, M.A. With additions by THOMAS SOUTHWELL, F.Z.S., HENRY STEVENSON, F.L.S., and ALFRED NEWTON, M.A., F.R.S.

Seals and Whales of the British Seas.
By THOMAS SOUTHWELL, F.Z.S. 4to, cloth, elegant. Illustrated.

> "We commend Mr. Southwell's book to all lovers of marine natural history: as the most practical and compendious manual we have upon the subjects it deals with."—*Land and Water.*
> "Hitherto no separate work upon the marine mammalia of Great Britain has existed, and Mr. Southwell's book supplies a want, and is likely to be of great value in elucidating a branch of zoology which, though full of interest, is as yet but very imperfectly understood. Whales of various species are from time to time cast up at various points all round our coast, often in most inaccessible places. There has until now been no book by means of which any intelligent resident in the neighbourhood interested in natural history could make out what was the species of the animal, and thus record its occurrence at the locality, or save it from destruction, if a rarity. No doubt many valuable specimens are lost to science yearly from ignorance of their worth."—*Athenæum.*

London; Jarrold & Sons, 3, Paternoster Buildings.

Books for Presentation, Prizes, &c.

PUBLISHED AT 5s.

A Woman's Hand. By E. M. ELLIS. 8vo, cloth, elegant, 425 pages. With Frontispiece.

"This is a pleasantly written and interesting story."—*Nonconformist.*

"The narrative is one of continuous movement and striking but natural incident, the whole so dexterously managed that the reader's interest is sustained to the close of the volume."—*General Baptist Magazine.*

The Handbook of Natural History (Mammalia). For Teachers and Pupil Teachers in Schools, Colleges, &c.

By W. J. STERLAND, late Lecturer on Natural History at the Home and Colonial Training College, London. 8vo, cloth, 455 pages. With Frontispiece.

Bible Pictures and Bible Words. Twenty-four *Coloured* Pictures, explained in the very words of Scripture. Suitable for the Family or School. Mounted on Gilt Moulding to hang up, exhibiting one sheet at a time.

The Old Testament Series. 5s.
The New Testament Series. 5s.

A Supplement to the Flora of Norfolk.

By the REV. KIRBY TRIMMER, M.A. Cloth.

PUBLISHED AT 3s. 6d.

Stories Illustrating Scripture Texts. NEW BOOK. By MRS. HENRY B. PAULL. A Series of Eight Stories for the Young People of the Family, bearing upon domestic or family Life. Cloth, elegant. Frontispiece.

The Greatest is Charity. A Series of Eight Stories on the Attributes of Charity, described in the 4th, 5th, and 7th verses of the Thirteenth Chapter of St. Paul's First Epistle to the Corinthians. By MRS. HENRY B. PAULL. Frontispiece. Crown 8vo, cloth, elegant, 400 pages. (Or with gilt edges, 4s. 6d.)

By MRS. WALTER SEARLE.

Redcar Lee. A Tale. Frontispiece. Crown 8vo, cloth, gilt.

Sarah Deck's Victory. A Tale. Frontispiece. Crown 8vo, cloth, gilt.

Somebody and Nobody. A Tale. Frontispiece. Crown 8vo, cloth, gilt.

Paul Haddon. A Tale. Frontispiece. Crown 8vo, cloth, gilt. An excellent Book for Young Men.

London: Jarrold & Sons, 3, Paternoster Buildings.

Books for Presentation, Prizes, &c.

PUBLISHED AT 3s. 6d.

Paul Porter and His Brothers. By P. A. BLYTH, Author of "Merry and Grave; or, What's in a Name?" Frontispiece. Crown 8vo, cloth, gilt.

The Mother of the Wesleys. By the REV. J. KIRK. Portrait, crown 8vo. (Or with gilt edges, 4s. 6d.)

Ishmael: a Tale of Syrian Life. By MRS. J. B. WEBB, Author of "Naomi," &c. With Eight full-page Illustrations. Cloth, elegant.

Mother's Last Words. By MRS. SEWELL. With fourteen beautiful Illustrations, designed and etched on Copper. By A. D. L. Handsomely bound in cloth.

Our Home Work. A Book for Girls. By MRS. WIGLEY, late of the Normal College Schools, Cheltenham. With Recommendatory Note from the Authoress of "The Peep of Day," "Line upon Line," &c.

PUBLISHED AT 3s.

D'Aubigne's History of the Great Reformation of the Sixteenth Century in Germany, Switzerland, France, &c. Abridged for Young Persons from the complete edition, chiefly by the Original Translator. New Edition, 12mo, cloth. Frontispiece.

PUBLISHED AT 2s. 6d.

By The REV. W. HASLAM.

Building from the Top, and other Readings. True Tales of Conversion. Twelve full-page Illustrations. Cloth, elegant.

From Death unto Life; or, Twenty Years of My Ministry. Cloth, elegant. With Two full-page Illustrations.

Yet Not I; or, More Years of My Ministry. Cloth, elegant. With Two full-page Illustrations.

Full Salvation as Seen in Bunyan's Pilgrim's Progress. Cloth, elegant. With Frontispiece, and Forty Illustrations.

The Lord is Coming. A Plain Narrative of Prophetic Events in their Order.

London: Jarrold & Sons, 3, Paternoster Buildings.

Books for Presentation, Prizes, &c.

PUBLISHED AT 2s. 6d.

Mother's Last Words. By MRS. SEWELL. With Fourteen beautiful Illustrations on Wood, by some of the first artists of the day. Handsomely bound in cloth, gilt edges.

Thy Poor Brother. Letters to a Friend on Helping the Poor. By MRS. SEWELL, Author of "Mother's Last Words." 12mo, cloth.

Homely Ballads and Stories in Verse. By MRS. SEWELL, Author of "Mother's Last Words." Coloured Frontispiece. Cloth.

Pictures and Ballads of Lowly Life. Consisting of "MOTHER'S LAST WORDS," and "OUR FATHER'S CARE." 4to, boards, cloth back, ornamental sides, with Twelve full-page Coloured Illustrations by Kronheim.

The Observing Eye. Letters to Children on the Three Lower Divisions of Animal Life—Radiated, Articulated, and Molluscous. Numerous Woodcuts and Coloured Frontispiece. Fcap. 8vo, cloth.

Bunyan's Pilgrim's Progress. Complete Edition. With Illustrations. Cloth, extra gilt.

Historical Tales of Illustrious British Children. By AGNES STRICKLAND. Coloured Frontispiece and Illustrations. 12mo, cloth, gilt edges.

Julio; a Tale of the Vaudois. For Young Persons. By MRS. J. B. WEBB, Author of "Naomi," &c. Full-page Illustrations. Fcap. 8vo, cloth, bevelled boards.

John Snow's Wife, and other Stories. By REV. C. COURTENAY. Handsomely bound in cloth; 12 Illustrations. Contents:—John Snow's Wife; The Two Watchers; The Two Friends, or, Parting and Meeting; Five Black Bottles, or, Uncle Robert's Hamper; Squire Armitage and His Remedies for Intemperance; Doctor Sharp's Stories; Mrs. Crappit's Grievance, a Sequel to John Snow's Wife; Bartle, the Butler; Betsy Trollope's Jug; Private Short; Not Half a Man, or, Mark Rayton's Fall; John Bowling, Coachman.

Bible Pictures and Bible Words. Old Testament. Twenty-four Simple Narratives for the Family and School, in the words of Scripture. 12½ in. by 20 in., on Roller. An Edition of the above, beautifully Coloured, price 5s.; or mounted on 24 Boards and Varnished, price 24s.

Bible Pictures and Bible Words. New Testament. Same Prices as Old Testament.

London: Jarrold & Sons, 3, Paternoster Buildings.

PUBLISHED AT 2s.

Black Beauty. The Autobiography of a Horse. By ANNA SEWELL. Frontispiece. 12mo, cloth. 75th Thousand.

> "Had the Society for the Prevention of Cruelty to Animals published this, we should say it had published its *best work*. As it is, it would be difficult to conceive one more admirably suited to its purpose." — *Review*.

Clean Money; How it was Made, and What it Accomplished; or, the Birthdays of Peter Conyer and Josiah Marten. By MRS. CONRAN. Crown 8vo. Frontispiece.

Myrtles of Merrystone Mill (The). By Miss ONLEY. Crown 8vo. Frontispiece.

Little Gladness. By NELLIE HELLIS, Author of "Little King Davie." Crown 8vo. With Frontispiece.

Two Little Lives. By Miss D. RYLANDS, Author of "Alfred May," &c. Crown 8vo. With Frontispiece.

The previous 5 books are uniformly bound in cloth, elegant, and are admirably adapted for School Prizes.

The Mother's Crown Jewels. By MRS. C. BICKERSTETH WHEELER, Author of "Memorials of a Beloved Mother," &c. Crown 8vo, cloth. Frontispiece.

> "'The Mother's Crown Jewels' deals exclusively with the training of children, and does so in a thoroughly wise and sensible style." — *The Baptist*.
> "It would be a useful book for Mothers' Meetings." — *The Christian*.

The Art of Thriving; or, Thrift Lessons in Familiar Letters. By JOHN T. WALTERS, M.A., Rector of Norton. 2nd Edition, revised. Crown 8vo. Frontispiece.

> "We are glad to see a second edition of this most useful and wholesome little book. . . . Full of useful information on household economy, gardening, cooking, health, and the up-bringing of children, which would alone make it worth buying and keeping." — *The Spectator*.

Patience Hart's First Experience in Service. By MRS. SEWELL, Author of "Mother's Last Words," 9th Thousand. Frontispiece. Cloth.

Ballads for Children. Including "Mother's Last Words," "Our Father's Care," and "The Children of Summerbrook." By MRS. SEWELL. Coloured Frontispiece and Illustrations. Fcap. 8vo, cloth, bevelled boards.

London: Jarrold & Sons, 3, Paternoster Buildings.

PUBLISHED AT 2s.

Stories of England and Her Forty Counties.
By Mrs. Thomas Geldart. Woodcuts and Coloured Frontispiece, 12mo, cloth.

Stories of Ireland and Its Four Provinces.
By Mrs Thomas Geldart. Woodcuts and Coloured Frontispiece, 12mo, cloth.

Stories of Scotland and Its Adjacent Islands.
By Mrs. Thomas Geldart. Woodcuts and Coloured Frontispiece, 12mo, cloth.

Working Together for Good; or, The Heir of Hazlewood. Coloured Frontispiece. Cloth. (Or cloth, bevelled boards, gilt edges.)

Our World: Its Rocks and Fossils. A Simple Introduction to Geology. By Mrs. Wright, Author of "The Observing Eye," &c., &c. 8th Edition, cloth. Illustrated.

Our World: Its Cities, Peoples, Mountains, Seas, and Rivers. By Edward Farr, F.S.A. Cloth. 100 Illustrations.

The Gipsy's Secret; or, Deb's Revenge, and What Came of it. By Mrs. Bewsher. Illustrated. 12mo, cloth.

Netty Moseley; or, Ears, and How to Use Them. By the Author of "Kenneth Forbes." Illustrated. 12mo, cloth.

Humphrey Merton; or, The Widow's Sons. Illustrated. 12mo, cloth.

Talks about Animals. By Uncle Robert. With upwards of Sixty Illustrations. 12mo, cloth.

Emily Milman; or, The Little Sunbeam of the Farmhouse. Illustrated. 12mo, cloth.

The Happy Village, and How it Became So. By Maria Wright. Illustrated. 12mo, cloth.

Ellen French. Passages from the Life of a Worker. By Aunt Evergreen. Frontispiece. 12mo, cloth.

London: Jarrold & Sons, 3, Paternoster Buildings.

PUBLISHED AT 2s.

What Mean Ye by This Service? or, Old Testament Sacrifices Explained: showing their Typical Meaning and Fulfilment in our Lord Jesus Christ. Illustrated. 12mo, cloth.

Bible Stories of the Old and New Testament. For Children from Ten to Thirteen years of age. By the REV. BOURNE HALL DRAPER. With Illustrations and Coloured Frontispiece. 16mo, cloth.

Mary and Her Mother. Scripture Stories for very Young Children. By MRS. ANDREW REED. Illustrations and Coloured Frontispiece. 16mo, cloth.

Early Days of Gospel Light; or, Events in the Lives of the Apostles. For Young People. By the Author of "The Prince of Peace." Illustrations and Coloured Frontispiece. 16mo, cloth.

PUBLISHED AT 1s. 6d.

Free England; or, Old Stories of the English Parliament. By MISS H. E. BOOTH. 8vo, cloth. With Frontispiece.

Kitty and Her Queen. By MISS ONLEY. 8vo, cloth. Frontispiece.

The Story of the Two Margarets. By EMMA MARSHALL, Author of "Katie's Work," "Rose Bryant," &c. Crown 8vo. cloth.

Joe Jasper's Troubles, and other Stories. By the Rev. CHARLES COURTENAY. 8vo, cloth. Twelve Illustrations.

The Flower Show at Fairley Court. By the REV. JAMES M. RUSSELL, Curate of the Abbey Church, Hexham.

The False Key, and other Stories. By J. W KIRTON, LL.D., Author of "Buy your own Cherries."

The Squire's Hat, and other Stories. By the Rev. JAMES M. RUSSELL, Curate of the Abbey Church, Hexham. 12 Illustrations.

London: Jarrold & Sons, 3, Paternoster Buildings.

Books for Presentation, Prizes, &c.

PUBLISHED AT 1s. 6d.

Plain Words on Temperance. Twenty-four Interesting Sketches, by the REV. CHARLES COURTENAY. Twenty-four Illustrations.

Gone to the Bottom. Twenty-four Interesting Sketches, and 24 Illustrations.

Half-Hour Temperance Readings (Series I.) By the REV. CHARLES COURTENAY. Cloth, 8vo. Twelve full-page Illustrations.

Half-Hour Temperance Readings (Series II.) By various Popular Authors. Cloth, 8vo. Twelve full-page Illustrations.

These books are eminently adapted for Reading at Mothers' & Cottage Meetings.

The Childhood of Distinguished Women. By SELINA BOWER. Six Illustrations, cloth, elegant.

Mabel's School Days. By Mrs. H. B. PAULL. Author of "The Greatest is Charity," &c. Frontispiece, Crown 8vo, cloth.

The Schoolboy Days of Eustace Lambert. A True Story. By FRANK PADDON. Frontispiece, 12mo, cloth.

Nothing too Simple for God. By LOUISE ERNESTINA. Frontispiece, Fcap. 8vo, cloth.

Faithful in Little. A Tale for Young Women. By Mrs. HEAD. Coloured Frontispiece, 12mo, cloth.

Roger's Apprenticeship; or, Five Years of a Boy's Life. By EMMA MARSHALL. Frontispiece, Crown 8vo, cloth.

Fred Williams. A Tale for Boys. Frontispiece, Crown 8vo, cloth.

The Little Gardeners. An Allegory for Children. 12mo, cloth. (Or cloth, gilt edges, 2s.)

Stories of the Early Christians. 12mo, cloth.

The Life of a Plant. "Science for the Household." Frontispiece, Fcap. 8vo, cloth.

Mother's Trials and Triumphs, and other Tales. For Fathers and Mothers. Fcap. 8vo, cloth, Coloured Frontispiece.

London: Jarrold & Sons, 3, Paternoster Buildings.

Books for Presentation, Prizes, &c.

PUBLISHED AT 1s. 6d.

Twilight Verses. By Mrs. DANIEL TOMKINS, Author of "Hymns for Quiet Hours."

Home Happiness, and other Tales. Fcap. 8vo, cloth. Coloured Frontispiece.

When to Say "No!" and other Tales. For Working Men. Fcap. 8vo, cloth. Coloured Frontispiece.

The Happy Life, and other Tales. For Young Women. Fcap. 8vo, cloth. Coloured Frontispiece.

How to Rise in the World, and other Tales. For Young Men. Fcap. 8vo, cloth. Coloured Frontispiece.

Starting in Life, and other Tales. For Boys and Girls. Fcap. 8vo, cloth. Coloured Frontispiece.

The Poetry of Home and School Life. Fcap. 8vo, cloth. Coloured Frontispiece.

The Pathway of Health. Fcap. 8vo, cloth. Coloured Frontispiece.

Marriage Bells, and other Tales. For Young Men and Women. Fcap. 8vo, cloth. Coloured Frontispiece.

Home, Sweet Home! and other Tales. Fcap. 8vo, cloth. Coloured Frontispiece.

Popular Readings. Fcap. 8vo, cloth. Coloured Frontispiece.

Tales in Rhyme. Fcap. 8vo, cloth. Coloured Frontispiece.

A True Briton, and other Tales. Fcap. 8vo, cloth. Coloured Frontispiece.

Do it with Thy Might; or, Our Work in the World. Addressed to those who ask, "What shall we do?" 18mo, cloth.

Sayings about Friendship. By the Author of "Do it with Thy Might." 18mo, cloth.

Memorable Days for Me and Mine. Cloth, gilt edges. (Or in roan, morocco, or calf, 2s. 6d.)

Here a Little and There a Little; or, Daily Manna for the Lambs of Christ's Fold. By a Mother. Frontispiece, 18mo, cloth.

London: Jarrold & Sons, 3, Paternoster Buildings.

Books for Presentation, Prizes, &c.

PUBLISHED AT 1s.

"Buy Your Own Cherries!" and other Tales. By J. W. Kirton, LL.D.

"Mother's Last Words," "Our Father's Care," &c. By Mrs. Sewell.

The Royal Brothers. By Agnes Strickland.

Guthred, the Widow's Slave. By Agnes Strickland.

Katie's Work. By Emma Marshall.

The Little Forester and His Friend. A Ballad. By Mrs. Sewell.

Stories from English History. By M. J. Wilkin.

Stories of Home Life. By Mrs. Brighton. Illustrated, 12mo, cloth.

Davie Blake, the Sailor. By Mrs. Sewell, Author of "Mother's Last Words." Illustrated, 8vo. (Or in cloth, 1s. 6d.)

Children of Summerbrook. Scenes of Village Life, in Simple Verse. By Mrs. Sewell, Author of "Mother's Last Words." Frontispiece. Fcap. 8vo, limp cloth.

Homely Ballads for the Working-Man's Fireside. By Mrs. Sewell. Fcap. 8vo, limp cloth. (Or with Coloured Frontispiece, cloth, 1s. 6d.)

Stories in Verse, for the Street and Lane. By Mrs. Sewell. Fcap. 8vo, limp cloth. (Or with Coloured Frontispiece, cloth, 1s. 6d.)

The Rose of Cheriton. By Mrs. Sewell. Fcap. 8vo, cloth. (Or in paper covers, 6d.)

Mother's Last Words. By Mrs. Sewell. Coloured Illustrations by Kronheim. 4to Picture Book. Coloured Wrapper.

Rose Bryant. Passages in her Maiden and Married Life. By Emma Marshall. Frontispiece, Fcap. 8vo, cloth.

London: Jarrold & Sons, 3, Paternoster Buildings.

Books for Presentation, Prizes, &c.

PUBLISHED AT 1s.

JARROLDS' SHILLING LIBRARY.

Black Beauty: His Grooms and Companions. The Autobiography of a Horse. By ANNA SEWELL.

The Art of Thriving; or, Thrift Lessons in Familiar Letters. By the Rev. J. T. WALTERS, M.A., Rector of Norton.

The Mother's Crown Jewels. By Mrs. C. BICKERSTETH WHEELER.

Clean Money: How it was Made, and what it Accomplished; or, the Birthdays of Peter Conyer and Josiah Marten. By Mrs. CONRAN.

Little Gladness. By NELLIE HELLIS, Author of "Little King Davie."

Two Little Lives. By Miss D. RYLANDS.

The Myrtles of Merrystone Mill. By Miss ONLEY.

Thy Poor Brother. By Mrs. SEWELL, Author of "Mother's Last Words."

The New Home; or, Wedded Life, its Duties, Cares, and Pleasures. Frontispiece, Fcap. 8vo, cloth.

The Peace Maker and the Mischief Maker. Frontispiece, 12mo, cloth.

Happy Half-Hours with the Bible; or, Mary Jane and Bertie. By AUNT EMILY. For a Mother, with her little Children. 18mo, cloth.

Lyrics for Little Ones. Frontispiece, 18mo, cloth.

Things of Every-Day Use. What they Are, Where they Come From, and How they are Made. 12mo, cloth.

Mother's Book of Health, and How to Manage a Baby. Frontispiece, 18mo, cloth.

London: Jarrold & Sons, 3, Paternoster Buildings.

Books for Presentation, Prizes, &c.

PUBLISHED AT 1s.

The Young Child's Gospel. In Verse, with Prayers and Hymns for Children. Coloured Frontispiece, 12mo, cloth.

Half-Hour Temperance Readings. By CHARLES COURTENAY. (In paper, 6d.)

Memorable Days for Me and Mine. Diary. Interleaved. Cloth. (Or in cloth, gilt edges, 1s. 6d.; morocco, roan or calf, 2s. 6d.)

Two Dear Little Feet. By Mrs. McFALL. Frontispiece, 12mo, cloth.

PUBLISHED AT 9d.

By Mrs. H. B. PAULL.

Mabel Berrington's Faith. "Let us not be weary in well-doing, for in due season we shall reap if we faint not."

Aunt Ellen's Success. "Whom the Lord loveth He chasteneth."

Constance Somerville. "Even a child is known by his doings, whether his work be pure and whether it be right."

The Vicar's Children. "In all thy ways acknowledge Him, and He will direct thy steps."

Horace Brereton's Discovery. "Set a watch, O Lord, before my mouth, keep the doors of my lips."

Walter Stanley's Essay. "Before honour is humility."

The Two Homes. "Let them learn first to show piety at home."

Philip Thornton's Legacy. "In everything give thanks."

Just Saved. The Story of Tom's Troubles. By HARRIET BOULTWOOD, Author of "Isidora," &c.

My Teacher's Gift. For Girls. Frontispiece, 18mo, cloth. A suitable Present for Sunday School Girls.

London: Jarrold & Sons, 3, Paternoster Buildings.

Books for Presentation, Prizes, &c.

PUBLISHED AT 9d.

My Teacher's Gift. For Boys. Frontispiece, 18mo, cloth. A suitable Present for Sunday School Boys.

Tales of the Work-room. The Sisters. By Mrs. CURTIS. Frontispiece, 18mo, cloth.

Consideration; or, How we can Help One Another. By EMMA MARSHALL. Coloured Frontispiece, 18mo, cloth.

Lessons about God. For very Young Children. By SOPHIA SINNETT. Coloured Frontispiece, 18mo, cloth.

PUBLISHED AT 6d.

My Text Book. A Text of Scripture with Appropriate Poetry for Every Day in the Year. Cloth, gilt edges.

Whisperings of the Soul. Sacred Poems. By HARRIET ROBBREDS. Cloth, gilt edges.

The Morning Repast. Being Daily Meditations and Hymns for a Month. Cloth, gilt edges.

Elizabeth Fry's Text Book. Texts for Every Day in the Year. Principally Practical and Devotional. Cloth, gilt edges.

Hymns for Quiet Hours. By Mrs. TOMKINS. Cloth, gilt edges.

The Martyr's Tree. By Mrs. SEWELL. 12mo, cloth.

The Mother's Sabbath Month. Hymns and Meditations for a Mother during her Month of Convalescence. 12mo, cloth.

Roger Wright's Fortune. By A. B. K.

London: Jarrold & Sons, 3, Paternoster Buildings.